Remembering Babylon

Remembering Babylon

David Malouf

PANTHEON BOOKS   NEW YORK

All rights reserved under International and Pan-American
Copyright Conventions. Published in the United States
by Pantheon Books, a division of Random House, Inc.,
New York. Originally published earlier in 1993 in the
United Kingdom by Chatto & Windus Ltd., London,
and in Canada by Alfred A. Knopf Canada, Toronto.

Library of Congress Cataloging-in-Publication Data

Malouf, David, 1934–
Remembering Babylon / David Malouf.
p.   cm.
ISBN 0-679-42724-4
1. Frontier and pioneer life—Australia—Fiction.
2. Australian aborigines—Fiction.   I. Title.
PR9619.3.M265R4   1993

823—dc20   93-7888
                                                       CIP

Manufactured in the United States of America

9   8   7   6   5   4   3   2

Whether this is Jerusalem or Babylon we know not.

WILLIAM BLAKE: *The Four Zoas*

Strange shapes and void afflict the soul
And shadow to the eye
A world on fire while smoke seas roll
And lightnings rend the sky

The moon shall be as blood the sun
Black as a thunder cloud
The stars shall turn to blue and dun
And heaven by darkness bowed
Shall make sun dark and give no day
When stars like skys shall be
When heaven and earth shall pass away
Wilt thou Remember me

JOHN CLARE

1

ONE DAY IN the middle of the nineteenth century, when settlement in Queensland had advanced little more than halfway up the coast, three children were playing at the edge of a paddock when they saw something extraordinary. They were two little girls in patched gingham and a boy, their cousin, in short pants and braces, all three barefooted farm children not easily scared.

They had little opportunity for play but had been engaged for the past hour in a game of the boy's devising: the paddock, all clay-packed stones and ant trails, was a forest in Russia – they were hunters on the track of wolves.

The boy had elaborated this scrap of make-believe out of a story in the fourth grade Reader; he was lost in it. Cold air burned his nostrils, snow squeaked underfoot; the gun he carried, a good sized stick, hung heavy on his arm. But the girls, especially Janet, who was older than he was and half a head taller, were bored. They had no experience of snow, and wolves did not interest them. They complained and dawdled and he had to exert all his gift for fantasy, his will too, which was stubborn, to keep them in the game.

They had a blue kelpie with them. He bounced along with his tongue lolling, excited by the boy's solemn concentration but puzzled too that he could get no sense of what they were after: the idea of wolf had not been transmitted to him. He danced around the little party, sometimes in front, sometimes to the side, sniffing close to the earth, raising his moist eyes in hope of instruction, and every now and then, since he was young and easily distracted, bounding away after the clippered insects that sprang up as they approached, or a grasshopper that rose with a ponderous whirring and rolled sideways from his jaws. Then suddenly he did get the scent. With a yelp of pure delight he shot off in the direction of their boundary fence, and the children, all three, turned away to see what he had found.

Lachlan Beattie felt the snow melt at his feet. He heard a faint far-off rushing, like wind rolling down a tunnel, and it took him a moment to understand that it was coming from inside him.

In the intense heat that made everything you looked at warp and glare, a fragment of ti-tree swamp, some bit of the land over there that was forbidden to them, had detached itself from the band of grey that made up the far side of the swamp, and in a shape more like a watery, heat-struck mirage than a thing of substance, elongated and airily indistinct, was bowling, leaping, flying towards them.

A black! That was the boy's first thought. We're being raided by blacks. After so many false alarms it had come.

The two little girls stood spellbound. They had given a gasp, one sharp intake of breath, then forgotten to breathe out. The boy too was struck but had begun to recover. Though he was very pale about the mouth, he did what his manhood required him to do. Holding fast to the stick, he stepped resolutely in front.

But it wasn't a raid, there was just one of them; and the thing, as far as he could make it out through the sweat in his eyes and its flamelike flickering, was not even, maybe, human. The stick-like legs, all knobbed at the joints, suggested a wounded waterbird, a brolga, or a human that in the manner of the tales they told one another, all spells and curses, had been *changed* into a bird, but only halfway, and now, neither one thing nor the other, was hopping and flapping towards them out of a world over there, beyond the no-man's-land of the swamp, that was the abode of everything savage and fearsome, and since it lay so far beyond experience, not just their own but their parents' too, of nightmare rumours, superstitions and all that belonged to Absolute Dark.

A bit of blue rag was at its middle from which sleeves hung down. They swung and signalled. But the sticks of arms above its head were also signalling, or beating off flies, or licks of invisible flame. Ah, that was it. It was a scarecrow that had somehow caught the spark of life, got down from its pole, and now, in a raggedy, rough-headed way, was stumbling about over the blazing earth, its leathery face scorched black, but with hair, they saw, as it bore down upon them, as sun-bleached and pale-straw coloured as their own.

Whatever it was, it was the boy's intention to confront it. Very sturdy and purposeful, two paces in front of his cousins, though it might have been a hundred yards in the tremendous isolation he felt, and with a belief in the power of the weapon he held that he knew was impossible and might not endure, he pushed the stick into his shoulder and took his stance.

The creature, almost upon them now and with Flash at its heels, came to a halt, gave a kind of squawk, and leaping up onto the top rail of the fence, hung there, its arms outflung as if preparing for flight. Then the ragged mouth gapped.

'Do not shoot,' it shouted. 'I am a B-b-british object!'

It was a white man, though there was no way you could have known it from his look. He had the mangy, half-starved look of a black, and when, with a cry, he lost his grip on the rail and came tumbling at their feet, the smell of one too, like dead swamp-water; and must have been as astonished as they were by the words that had jumped out of his mouth because he could find no more of them. He gaped, grinned, rubbed his side, winced, cast his eyes about in a hopeless way, and when he found speech again it was a complaint, against himself perhaps, in some whining blackfeller's lingo.

The boy was incensed. The idea of a language he did not know scared him. He thought that if he allowed the man to go on using it, he would see how weak they were and get the advantage of them. He jerked the stick in the direction of the man's heart. 'Stop that,' he yelled. 'Just steik yur mooth.'

The man, responding to the truculence of the boy's tone, began to crawl about with his nose in the dust. The boy relaxed – That's better, he thought – and even Flash, seeing now that the fellow was prepared to be docile, stopped yapping and began to tongue the stranger's knees.

The man was not keen on it. With a childish whimper he began to hop about, trying to shake the dog off. Lachlan, disturbed and a little disgusted by this display of unmanliness but eager to show that he could be a generous victor, as well as a stern one, called Flash off. 'Ge on wi' ye,' he told the fellow in as gruff a voice as he could manage, and soon had his prisoner going, but at a hobbling gait – one of his legs was shorter than the other. He ordered his cousins to keep back, and in the glow of his new-found mastery they let themselves be led.

After a time the man began to grunt, then to gabble as if in protest, but when Lachlan put the stick into his spine, moved on faster, producing sounds of such eager submissiveness that the boy's heart swelled. He had a powerful sense of the springing of his torso from the roots of his belly. He had known nothing like this! He was bringing a prisoner in. Armed with nothing, too, but his own presumptuous daring and the power of make-believe.

So the little procession made its way to where the girls' father was ringbarking in the gully below their hut.

*

4

An hour later news of the affair had spread all through the settlement. A crowd had gathered to see this specimen of – of what? What was he?

They stood in the heat, which was overpowering at this time of the day, and stared.

Distractions were unusual up here; even the Syrian pedlar did not trouble to come so far. They were isolated, at the end of the line.

Apart from their scattered holdings, the largest of which was forty acres, there was nothing to the settlement but a store and post office of unpainted weatherboard, with a verandah and a dog in front of it that was permanently asleep but if kicked would shift itself, walk five steps, then flop.

Opposite the store was a corrugated iron shack, a shanty-pub, unlicensed as yet, with hitching posts and a hollowed log that served as a trough.

The area between, the open space where they now stood, was part of a road perhaps, since horses and carts went back and forth upon it, and women in sunbonnets, and barefoot youths who, with nothing to do in the evening, came to sit with their feet up on the rails of the verandah and tell raw jokes, practise their spitting, and flick cigarette butts with a hiss into the trough. It was not yet a street, and had no name.

The nearest named place, Bowen, was twelve miles off, but the twelve miles meant that they were only lightly connected to it, and even more lightly to what *it* was connected to: the figure in an official uniform who had given it his name and the Crown he represented, which held them all, a whole continent, in its grip.

'He's an ugly-lookin' bloke, aren't you, eh? Faugh! Don't 'e stink, but!'

'Dumb. I reckon 'e's dumb.'

5

'No he's no'! He spoke t' me. Don't shoot, he said, didn' ye, eh? Don't shoot! Don't shoot!'

The man, recognising the words as his own, showed his blackened teeth, which were ground down to the stumps, and did a little lopsided dance, then looked foolish.

'Don't shoot,' the boy repeated, and held the stick up to his shoulder. One of the smaller children laughed.

'Ah'm the wan he kens,' the boy repeated. He was determined to keep hold of the bit of glory he had won. 'Don't you, eh? Eh? Ah'm the wan.' With a boisterous persistence that kept him very nearly breathless, he scampered off to collar newcomers, but always dashed back to be at the man's side, at the centre of their gaze.

For a moment back there, seeing himself as these grown-ups might see him, a mere kid, a twelve-year-old and small for his age, he had felt a wave of anxiety at how shaky his power might be. But he'd recovered – all his recoveries were like this, as quick as the fits of despondency he fell into – and was fired once more with the excitement of the thing. The air crackled around him. He shone. Over and over, in words that each time he repeated them made him see the event, and himself too, in a light more vivid, more startling, he told how it had happened: how the fellow had come flying at the fence 'as if an airmy o' fiends were aifter him', and when he leapt up onto the rail, his words.

The words were what mattered most to the boy. By changing the stick he held into what his gesture had claimed for it, they had changed him too, and he did not want, now, to change back. So long as he kept talking, he thought, and the others listened, he would not.

Janet McIvor, who had also been there and seen all that occurred, though no one seemed interested in her version, was surprised that he was allowed to get away with it; their father wasn't always so easy. But he and their mother seemed as gawpingly awe-struck as the rest. Neither of them had made the least move to bring him down.

The fact was that the event itself, which was so unusual and unexpected, had made the boy, since he claimed so large a part in it, as strange almost to their customary view of him as the half-caste or runaway. Something impressive and mysterious set the two figures, Lachlan Beattie as much as the straw-topped half-naked savage, in a dimension where they appeared unreachable. So the boy simply had his way till his aunt, who had never seen him in such a state, darting this way and that like an actor on a stage, out of a fear that he might be about to explode under her very eyes, told him for heaven's sake to cool down, and his uncle, woken as if from a dream, stepped in and took a hand to him.

He looked about him, open-eyed at last, rubbed the side of his head where his uncle's hand had come down, and was again just a wiry twelve-year-old. The runaway, who might, they now thought, be some sort of simpleton, was alarmed at this outburst and began to moan.

'Me and Meg found him, just as much as Lachlan,' Janet McIvor put in, seizing her opportunity, but no one paid heed. 'And anyway, it was Flash.'

'Oh for heaven's sake, lassie,' her mother told her, 'dinnae you start.'

Meanwhile the man stood waiting. For what?

For one of them to start something.

But where *could* you start with an odd, unsettled fellow who, beyond what the boy Lachlan had heard him shout, had not a word you could make sense of in the English tongue; a pathetic, muddy-eyed, misshapen fellow, all fidgets, who seemed amazed by them – as if *they* were the curiosities here – and kept laughing and blinking.

He was a man who had suffered a good deal of damage. There were scorch marks on his chest and arms where he had rolled into a camp fire, and signs that he had, at one time or another, taken a fair bit of knocking about. One of his eyebrows was missing. Strange how unimportant eyebrows can be, so long as there are two of them. It gave his face a smudged appearance. He had the baffled, half-expectant look of a mongrel that has been often whipped but still turns to the world, out of some fund of foolish expectancy, as a source of scraps as well as torments.

His joints were swollen and one leg was shorter than the other and a little twisted. When he got excited he jerked about as if he was being worked by strings, one or two of which had snapped. He screwed his face up, grinned, looked interested, then, in a lapse of courage or concentration, went mute and glanced about as if he did not know, suddenly, how he had got there or where he was.

The country he had broken out of was all unknown to them. Even in full sunlight it was impenetrably dark.

To the north, beginning with the last fenced paddock, lay swamp country, bird-haunted marshes; then, where the great spine of the Dividing Range rose in ridges and shoals of mist, rainforest broken by sluggish streams.

The land to the south was also unknown. Settlement up here proceeded in frog-leaps from one little coastal place to the next. Between lay tracts of country that no white man had ever entered. It was disturbing, that: to have unknown country behind you as well as in front. When the hissing of the lamp died out the hut sank into silence. A child's murmuring out of sleep might keep it human for a moment, or a rustling of straw; but what you were left with when the last sleeper settled was the illimitable night, where it lay close over the land. You lay listening to the crash of animals through its underbrush, the crack, like a snapped bone, of a ringbarked tree out in a paddock, then its muffled fall; or

and turned away. Gemmy, his brow furrowed, had begun to skip about on one leg. Little whimpering sounds came from him.

'He wants it back,' one of the smaller children said dreamily out of her own experience, and looked about, suddenly shy at having spoken.

'He does too. The bairn's right. Give it 'im back.'

Jock McIvor, whose hands it had come to, passed the rag back, and the fellow grinned and hugged it to his chest but made no attempt to restore it to where it would do most good. This was too much for Jim Sweetman. 'For God's sake, man,' he exploded, 'cover yourself.'

Jim Sweetman, an ex-blacksmith, was a man who was accorded a good deal of respect among them. He was a big, stern-faced fellow who in all weathers wore a flannel vest out of which grey wire crawled. He disapproved of swearing and had only one oath of his own, which was 'By Godfrey', but was a dancer with the lightness of a man half his weight and half his age and was often seen with his three-year-old granddaughter on his arm, bouncing her up and down to the tune of a waltz. He did not impose his authority and no word of rebuke ever passed his lips, but there were few among them who did not shrink from the image they got of themselves when Jim Sweetman, with a look of sadness rather than scorn, fixed them for a moment with his gaze and turned regretfully away.

He had taken no part in the guessing game – no pleasure either. A lot of grown men and women idling about, grinning and shouting while a plain savage, or marionette or imbecile, jigged about and played up to them. And all this with not a stitch to cover him! Bad enough if he was what he appeared to be, a poor savage, but if he was a white man it was horrible. 'Somebody get the fellow some proper covering,' he thundered when it was clear that no one else had seen the need or was willing to forgo the spectacle long enough

13

to remedy it. Flushed with shame, he snatched the rag from the man's hands, pushed it at him, and pointed, then looked away. The man grinned. Very complaisantly he knotted the thing, but in an ineffectual manner, at his waist.

But now he was off on a new game. He had something else to show.

He banged his head with the flat of his hand and 'H-h-head' he hooted, then looked alarmed as if the word had popped out without his will. They watched, waited for more, but he was stopped for the moment.

It was the stammer. It belonged to someone he had thought was gone, lost, and here it was on his lips again. It had come back at the moment, up there on the fence, when he first found words in his English tongue. A weakness that was inseparable, perhaps, from the tongue itself. It damp-ened him a little. It set him back. But he swallowed hard and defied it.

'Nose' he yelled, clasping his own, and laughing outright at the ease with which he found the word and got it out. 'Arm! M-m-mouth! Ear!' He was shouting now for his own sake rather than to demonstrate anything, half drunk with what kept coming.

It was as if the language these people spoke was an atmos-phere they moved in. Just being in their proximity gave him access to it. He breathed it up out of the air between them, snatched the words like buttons off their shirts, or hairs out of their beards. 'B-b-beard' he yelled – again, it was with him now, and would not go away – 'foot', holding one up and dancing awkwardly on the other; then, with an appeal to what he knew was the comic side of things, 'arse', and slapped his meagre buttocks.

One or two of the children laughed and clapped their hands over their mouths, all eyes. The smallest among them, their young thin faces very grave and intent, looked up to see how their parents would take it and, when no protest

14

appeared, wondered if some new set of rules was in operation, and this blackfeller's arrival among them was to be the start of something.

And now, with a spurt of excited energy, he lunged into the crowd, and before anyone could prevent it, had wrested a hammer from one of the onlookers, a hulking, harelipped youth, Hec Gosper, who in the first shock of the assault, and under the suspicion of some sort of native treachery, made the mistake of trying to wrench it back. The fellow was stronger than he looked; he hung on and a struggle ensued. They wrestled for the hammer, pulling this way and that, till one or two of the bystanders started barracking, and Hector, with a baffled look, and the realisation that he was being made ridiculous, gave up.

A cheerful youth but very sensitive of his standing, he felt the others had let him down. Some of the barracking had been for the black.

He stood with his shirt rucked up behind and dragged his forearm across his brow. The harelip meant that he had had to fight hard in the past not to be taunted. He was incensed now that the accident of his arriving on the scene with a hammer should once again make a victim of him. With a savage gesture, he pushed his shirt back into his pants and stood nursing his wounds.

But all the man wanted, it seemed, was to show that he knew how the thing was used. Holding an imaginary nail very daintily between forefinger and thumb, he raised the hammer and made a show of belting it in.

'A nail,' someone shouted, not realising that the earlier game was ended.

The man knocked in another nail, then, looking very pleased with himself, and with great solemnity, restored the tool to its offended owner, attempting as he did to pat the youth affectionately on the shoulder.

'Get offa me,' the boy hissed, and jerked his elbow up under the nigger's chin.

The details of his story were pieced together the following afternoon from facts that were, as he told them, all out of their proper order, and with so many gaps of memory, and so much dislocation between what he meant to convey and the few words he could recover of his original tongue, that they could never be certain, later, how much of it was real and how much they had themselves supplied from tales they already knew, since he was by no means the first white man to have turned up like this after a spell among the blacks.

It was the minister, Mr Frazer, who examined him, in the hot little one-roomed schoolhouse, and the schoolmaster, George Abbot, who did the writing up.

The man was squeezed into a desk in the front row, with Mr Frazer opposite. George Abbot sat at his usual place, at the table on the dais, in front of a greenish blackboard cloudy with chalk dust and covered with sums in long division.

For the first half hour Lachlan Beattie was present. Since a kind of understanding had been struck between the man and his earliest interpreter, Mr Frazer thought things might go easier if he was there. But the boy was so bumptious, so ready to interrupt and contradict and take upon himself the main part of the proceedings, that George Abbot, who had to deal with him five days a week and was not inclined to be patient, told him to sit still and speak only when he was invited. Even Mr Frazer agreed at last that it might be better if he went back to his companions. They, in their delight at any sort of show, were hanging about in troops on the verandah, and whenever events inside showed a spark of action, jostled and shoved in the window frame.

Deeply humiliated before so many witnesses, who were only too happy to see him brought down, Lachlan departed, but comforted himself with the thought that in dismissing him they had lost their one chance of getting at the truth. Only he, as yet, had any clear hold on what the fellow was trying to say. He watched now from the sill, with a little smirk of contempt for the minister's wrong guesses, which were many, and with the satisfaction, every now and then, of receiving from Gemmy a look of stricken appeal that he was impelled, with a shrug of his shoulders, to ignore.

The trouble was that Gemmy, in his childish eagerness to provide Mr Frazer with whatever it was he wanted to hear, leaped at every suggestion, and once his own meagre fund gave out was only too pleased to have Mr Frazer find words for him.

It was Mr Frazer's belief that the sympathy he felt for the man, which was very strong, gave him an infallible insight into what he was trying to get out. When the poor fellow knotted his brow, and gnawed his lip, and hummed and agonised, Mr Frazer, all his body hunched and drawn forward till he was practically breathing into the man's mouth, would offer syllables, words, anything to relieve the distress he felt at Gemmy's distress, so that they sat, at times, at a distance of just inches, hooting and shouting at one another; on Gemmy's side, odd bursts of sound, half-meanings at most; on the other, whole phrases that, whether or not they were quite what the man intended, found their way into what George Abbot set down.

'Yes sir, yes, that's it,' Gemmy would splutter, delighted, since the minister was, at having done so well, and Mr Frazer, another fierce struggle ended, would look relieved and say, 'Good, I thought that might be it.' With the tip of his forefinger on the fleshy place between his nostrils, he would consider a moment, then give George the sign to dip his pen and write.

A young man of just nineteen, in a jacket and tie, his nose peeled with sunburn, George Abbot resented the role he was

17

being forced to play in this pantomime, and the more so because Mr Frazer was in his eyes such a fool. He felt his authority was undermined by his being put to use, and in front of his own pupils too, as a mere clerk. When they surged in the window-space and would not be silenced by hard looks, he felt his temper rise and would have intervened to restore order; Mr Frazer was a man who did not inspire respect. But he dared not challenge the older man, despised himself for it, and resented the occasion all the more.

It was hot under the roof. He had a tendency to sweat. He hooked a finger under his collar, worked it round a little to ease the tightness, and while Mr Frazer once again put his questions, and agonised and prompted, and the man clenched his jaw and his knuckled fingers and hummed, let his gaze drift beyond the crowd of heads in the window-space to the stunned landscape, and in a dreamy way into its depths.

When one of his charges did this, he would, with stinging accuracy, fling an inch of chalk at his head, then make the culprit, still rubbing the smart of it and glaring under his greasy pudding bowl, kneel with his nose to the wall.

There was no one to fling chalk at him. Young enough to respond, as his pupils did, to the drowsiness that stole over your senses in the airless heat, and to the heaviness and constriction of his clothes, especially the thick cloth between his thighs, he found himself losing hold of Mr Frazer's voice. The thrumming of his blood was curiously at one with the shimmering, out there, of the landscape and the shrilling of insects, a sound so continuous, so dimly insistent in these late-summer days that it stilled the senses and drew you irresistibly into its own drawn-out –

'Ready George? George?'

He started.

'Ready sir.'

Drawing a handkerchief from his cuff, he mopped the

meat of his palm, then crumpled and replaced it, dipped his pen, and casting an amused glance over the happy couple, who had come to an end for the moment of their shouting and spluttering, bent his neck to the task. As each sheet was filled he passed it to the minister, and Mr Frazer, holding it at arm's length while Gemmy looked on blinking, read it through.

They came to the third sheet, and while Mr Frazer ran his eye over it, muttering a little, George Abbot made a pretence of examining his nib. A smile played on his lips.

Out of boredom, but also to set himself at a distance from the occasion and to register, if only in an obscure and indirect way, the contempt he felt at the minister's smugness, he had introduced into what he had just set down a phrase or two of his own.

Hidden away in Mr Frazer's orotund periods, they were an assertion of personality, of independence, of his refusal to be a mere tool. He waited to see if Mr Frazer would notice. When he did not, he resolved next time to be bolder. The imp of invention gave a gleeful kick in him and what he added now was not a change of phrasing but an alteration of fact – nothing blatant. The thought of this scrap of mistruth, deliberately introduced among so much that was mere guesswork on the minister's part, not to say sentimental fantasy, appealed to his sense of the absurd; he delighted in it, even if he was the only one who would ever know it was there. In this way he appropriated a little of the occasion to himself, stepped in and concealed himself, a sceptical shade, at this and that point of the minister's Colonial fairytale.

When all was done, and Mr Frazer had read over the half-dozen or more sheets and nodded his satisfaction, he invited Gemmy, who had been craning his neck to follow the proceedings, to take the sheets and handle them; out of a sense, a weird one George thought, but the minister did have these fits of weirdness, that in doing so the man might grasp a little of what they had been doing here and what the seven closely written pages represented.

To George's vast amusement, Gemmy, as he received the sheets, put on a solemn expression very like Mr Frazer's own, shuffled the pages according to his own taste, and holding them, as Mr Frazer had, at arm's length, and making the same little humphing sounds of grave approval, ran his eyes down one page, then the next. When this ritual was completed he raised the sheets to his nose and sniffed them, and might have been preparing, till Mr Frazer intervened, to lick and maybe swallow them. He looked puzzled when Mr Frazer gently took them back.

Mute now, but with his tongue making shy appearances at the corner of his mouth as if the tip of it was the real faculty of observation in him, he watched the sheaf of pages go into the pocket of the minister's coat, and continued to watch, believing perhaps that the magic they had been practising here was not yet over, and Mr Frazer, with a flourish, might bring them forth again, but in the shape this time of a plump white pigeon or a line of gaudy handkerchiefs.

This last conceit was the schoolmaster's, not Gemmy's, but was more accurate than he knew. Magic, as Gemmy understood it, had been the essence of the occasion.

He knew what writing was but had never himself learned the trick of it. As he handled the sheets and turned them this way and that, and caught the peculiar smell they gave off, his whole life was in his throat – tears, laughter too, a little – and he was filled with an immense gratitude. He had shown them what he was. He was known. Left alone with the sheets, to brood and sniff, the whole of what he was, *Gemmy*, might come back to him, and he began to plot, as he thought of his life out of sight there in the minister's pocket, how to steal it back.

It did not surprise him – it was the nature of magic – that

all that had happened to him, all his fortune good and bad, and so much sweat and pain, and miles travelled and bones picked and nights of freezing dew, and dreams, and dreams – all, over the long afternoon that he had glimpsed and recognised, glimpsed and shied away from, and intended and failed to tell, should be reduced now to what a man could hold in his hand and slip into a pocket; a few sheets in which, if he could only identify where they were among the squiggles, he might find Willett with his bristling red hair, and the rats, and old Crouch, now that he thought of it, and his daughter the silkie – had he mentioned that? Not Mosey and The Irish. He wouldn't want them in it. Not *them*.

He hugged himself. What came back to him was the strong-smelling, earth-smelling black stuff he had caught a whiff of when he held the papers to his nose.

Was that the smell of his life, his spirit, the black blood they had drained out of him? No wonder he felt weak.

All the events of his life, all that he had told and not told, and more, much more, now that it had begun to stir and move, which he was just beginning to recall, had been curled up in him like an old-man carpet snake. It was awake now. Lifting its blind head it was emerging coil on coil into the sun.

2

Lying half in salt and the warm wash of it, half in air that blistered. Eyelids so puffed with light that no more light struck through them, and what did blinded him. Nostrils crusted, the air without moisture between his lips, each shallow mouthful of it a flame in his throat.

All over him a flaking, and the flakes tiny creatures, clawed and with mouths, all light, that crawled into the cracks that had been opened in him, seeking bone. Only when a shadow of cloud passed over did the many mouths of the light desist.

Tries to hold it, the shadow; to make at least the memory of it last on his flesh, and cool and calm the furious activity all over the surface of him. But his mind lets the cloud slide away like everything else it has held. All that remains in his skull, behind the blind eyes, is sky, and that too burns, shakes out flame. Cloud after cloud rolls over, touches, cools, and is gone. Beyond hold.

The mob of naked women and gleaming, big-eyed children who found him washed up at low tide in their bay, stood with one foot set upon the other and clenched their brows.

What was it? A sea-creature of a kind they had never seen before from the depths beyond the reef? A spirit, a feeble one, come back from the dead and only half reborn?

The flesh was raw, covered with white flower-like ulcers where the salt had got in, opening mouths that as the soft water touched them lifted pale tentacles. Tiny crabs heaped and climbed over one another's soft-shelled backs, and heaved and glittered. One of the women tried to drive them off. Seething, they rose up in waves from under him, tumbling out of the folds of bark he was wrapped in, and with the sighing of a million tiny claws as the sand grains slipped under them, wheeled in a cloud over the bubbling sand.

The creature's eyes sprang open. They were of a milky colour; blank, maybe blind. The mob shifted closer.

The eyes were open upon something. Not us, they thought.

Not them, but some other world, or life, out of which the creature, whatever it was, sea-calf or spirit, was still emerging. They started, expecting as they watched to see some further transformation. The eyelids drooped and flickered. Now, they thought. It is letting go of that other life. It sees us. Now. The mouth opened, revealing a swollen tongue. But no change occurred.

Very timidly, as if fearful of exposing themselves to impiety, or of setting off some change in the creature other than the one it was slowly working towards, they lifted the loose husk that covered it, and found the silvered skin, the belly with its familiar indentation and knot (a flutter of excitement swept over them), and as the last encrustation of crabs broke up and his sea-attendants left him, the white worm of his prick. Again they murmured one to the other but remained puzzled and drew back.

He watched them. Let them do what they would with him. What struck him was the smell they gave off; or maybe it was the air of the place. Animal, unfamiliar. What he thought was: I am lost again, more lost than ever. It is not what I expected.

What he had expected, beyond so much flame, after so many days of burning, was Willett, rising up in an odour of char, with his eyebrows ablaze and his scorched boots hanging from their laces at his neck. The disappointment of it was like tears in his throat and choked him.

23

One of the older women sent a younger one off, and when she returned it was with water that sloshed from a gourd. They wetted his lips with it. He moaned, clutched, set his teeth to the lip of the thing, gulping. He kept his eyes fixed on them over the rim and they leaned forward to see him drink.

A little later, he could not say how long, he was no longer at the sea's edge, but in soft sand, in the shade of a shrub whose fan-like needles broke the light just inches from his face and fanned it with coolness. The huddle of women, chattering like birds, was moving away.

Later again he found himself in darkness not far from a fire where shadows flared. The smell of smoke pricked his nostrils – Ah, perhaps, after all!

The high treetops were filled with a buzzing which he thought the stars were making. How had he got here? Had someone carried him or had he dragged himself up the beach into the scrub, drawn by the sound of voices and the promise of company? For the voices he had heard were human. It was the humming breath of them, rising up in the clear night, that he had taken for stars.

After a moment, using his elbows, he began to push himself towards them and out into the firelight. Their many faces, touched with flame, turned towards him, mouths open, eyes staring, as the pale, wormlike figure inched towards them.

He squirmed into a sitting position and heard the gasp of their breath. Dropping forward, he raised himself on all fours; then, with an effort, staggering upright, held his hands out and began to whine in what he had learned, long ago, was a piteous manner – he did not think it would be less effective here than on the streets back home – and with a whole repertoire of gestures that were meant to engage and win them over, waggled his ears, pulled his mouth wide with a finger in each corner, producing at first only a kind of shocked silence in them, till the stillness was broken by a peal of laughter, then exploded in general hilarity.

They tossed him scraps, and fell still again as he sat with his head down and tore with his teeth at singed fur. Then he curled up just where he was and slept, and when he woke, all round him, under drifts of mist past the trunks of trees, they were preparing to leave.

He followed. At first at a distance, though one or two of them glanced back from time to time to see if he was still with them; then closer, till he made one of the loose mob of old folk, women mostly, who straggled in the rear.

They left a good space round him, but in a place where the forest thickened and it was almost dark, tried to elbow him off the track, then, when they saw that he was not to be got rid of, gave up. One old woman, with no sign of personal interest, as if he were a little white hairless thing that could not fend for itself, gave him a mouthful of seeds. Once again, half-fearful, they watched while he swallowed it. When they came to a halt at last and made camp, he claimed a place for himself in the second or third ring from the fire, and his neighbours, though wary, made no dispute.

So he began his life among them, doing what he had always done. It was all he knew. Since he had somehow found his way into the world, his object, like any other creature's, was to stay in it and by any means he could. He had a belly to be fed. In the days that followed he winkled out a place among them, made himself small, scouted about for this or that one he might attach himself to, looked droll, looked pathetic, and when he could not get what he wanted that way, would dart in under the half-playful, half-timorous cuffs, grab what he could and gobble it down before he was stopped. He was not put off by the occasional bruise.

He was a child, with a child's quick capacity to take things in and the street child's gift of mimicry. They were astonished at the swiftness with which he learned their speech, and once a thing had been pointed out to him, how keen his eyes were. Relying on a wit that was instinctive in him and had been sharpened under harder circumstances than these, he let himself be gathered into a world which, though he was alarmed at first by its wildness, proved no different in essence from his previous one, for all that it was, day after day, hot tracks over stone, and insect bites, and nights when you had to creep in under logs while the rain slushed, and long spells between one bellyful and the next.

Watching out for it, and for himself, he got into his mouth as much of its fat and flesh as he could manage, its names too, its breath. What kept you alive here was the one and the other, and they were inseparable: the creature with its pale ears raised and stiffened, sitting up alert in its life as you were in yours, and its name on your tongue. When it kicked its feet and gushed blood it did not go out of the world but had its life now in you, and could go in and out of your mouth forever, breath on breath, and was not lost, any more than the water you stooped to drink would cease to run because you gulped it down in greedy mouthfuls, then pissed it out.

Young enough to learn and to be shaped as if for the first time, he was young enough also to forget. He lost his old language in the new one that came to his lips. He had never in fact possessed more than the few hundred words that were immediately needful to him, to fill his belly or save his skin, having heard little in his short life but commands, curses, coarse endearments, the street talk he had learned to spit out like the rest, and such bits and pieces of something lighter – jokes, riddles, the words of a penny-gaff tune – that he had picked up from Willett, or at the beer shop while he was waiting on one foot for their ale to be drawn, and in his years at sea from the talk of sailors bent over a bit of darning in the swing of the foc's'le lamp or sprawling on deck. It was not enough to hold him.

As for things, nothing he had dealt with had been his own. He had stammered over most of them, b-b-boots, j-j-jug; his hold was buttery. Now they slipped away altogether, they dropped out of his life, and with them, and the words, went whatever thin threads had held them together and made up the fabric of his world.

Occasionally some object out of his old life would come floating back and bump against him. He would see it clearly enough, feel his hand clasping the handle of the jug or smell the dark-stained leather, but no word was connected to them, and when his mind reached for it, the object too went thin on him. He felt a kind of sadness that was like hunger, but of the heart, not the belly, and could only believe, since these things came to him only in fragments, that they belonged to the life of some other creature whose memory he shared, and which rose up at moments to shake him, then let him go.

In time his coming among them became another tale they told and he would listen to it with a kind of wonder, as if what they were recounting had happened ages ago, in a time beyond all memory, and to someone else. How, when they found him he had still been half-child, half-seacalf, his hair swarming with spirits in the shape of tiny phosphorescent crabs, his mouth stopped with coral; how, ash-pale and ghostly in his little white shirt, that long ago had rotted like a caul, he had risen up in the firelight and danced, and changed before their eyes from a sea-creature into a skinny human child.

He would listen, and in one part of himself, the part that belonged to their tribal life, he believed, but in some other part he did not. There was a different story, he thought, which was his alone and secret: which had another shape, and might need, for its telling, the words he had had in his

27

mouth when they first found him, and had lost; though not, he thought, forever.

He was accepted by the tribe but guardedly; in the droll, half-apprehensive way that was proper to an in-between creature.

No woman, for example, would have to do with him, and there were many objects in the camp that he was forbidden to touch. Their life was a cat's cradle of rights and restrictions; they all had objects, people too, that they must not look upon; but the restrictions on him were his alone, and the separation he felt, his questionable status, kept alive in him what he might otherwise have let go. When he stretched out in his place by the camp fire and his eyes and hands had nothing to engage them, the images that came, even if he could not grasp them, were as real as the fat in his mouth, or the familiar, distinctive odour of those who were stretched beside him.

'Boots' the darkness whispered – he caught only the breath of the word – and there they were: objects that made no sense here, that he saw propped up in front of a barred grate with flame in every crack of their leather, the tongues loose, the laces trailing, and the voice in the dark, very hoarse but not fierce, was Willett's, and there he was too, rising up out of them with his eyebrows blazing. Willett!

The others had their own explanation for these midnight hauntings. He was a tormented spirit. The cries he uttered in his sleep, the terrors that assailed him, were proof that although he had the look of a man, he was not one, not yet. A day would come when, fully arrived among them, he would let go of the other world.

His view was different. One day, he thought, I will turn around on some track deep in the scrub and *he* will be there, making fast towards me, not ghostly, in no way ghostly, and I will wait there for him to catch up, open a place for him to step into, and we will go on. He did not ask himself where.

In the meantime he was here, though where here was, and why he was in this place rather than another, was a mystery to him.

He approached this mystery at times, just touched it, and was uneasy. Mostly he let it alone. When the time comes, he told himself, it will approach me.

So when news drifted up from the south of spirits, white-faced, covered from head to foot in bark and riding four-footed beasts that were taller than a man, he was disturbed, and the desire to see these creatures, to discover what they were, plucked at him till he could not rest. In the company of an old woman who knew the country because she had grown up there, he set out to find them, but when they came to a part of it that she did not know, the woman turned back. He went on alone. Long before Lachlan Beattie and the two girls found him he had been skirting the edge of the settlement, living off the strange yet familiar country down there, and keeping watch from the cover of the scrub.

His first discovery was tracks of a kind that utterly puzzled him, then, in the middle of the path, a line of droppings, big, round, golden-dark with a sheen to them, about the size of a buzzard's egg, unlike the pellets of local creatures. Touched with a fearful curiosity, he got down on all fours and sniffed. A kind of clattering filled his head, and he glanced up, expecting to find himself in the narrow and noisy confines of – of what? What had he almost seen? It was gone again. Was that what he would find on the other side of the scrub?

He worried over the image, trying to catch again some detail that would make a picture, but it had been just a flash, mostly noise and a sense of panic in him. And all around, so clear that it filled all the spaces in him, was the familiar busyness of the scrub, a low, continuous rub and fret broken by bird calls, each of which brought a clear little body to his mind, flutterings, scurryings, the skirl of insects.

The next sign he came to was a red blanket thrown over a line. His heart leapt. But when he crept forward and whipped it aside there was only a blaze of grass heads, the bulk of a wooden hut, and standing in front of it, a little round-bellied naked child, rather unsteady on her white legs, and staring. She stood like that for a moment, puzzled, absorbed, then raised her fists to her eyes and howled.

Later, from another part of the scrub, he looked into a clearing, all raw timber and scattered leaves, and saw a bearded fellow in a blue shirt and braces who spat on his hands, took up a long-handled, bladed instrument, and stood preparing to swing it. He was amazed. A kind of meaning clung to the image in the same way that the clothes he was wearing clung to the man, and when the blade flashed and jarred against wood, it struck home in him. *Axe.*

The word flew into his head as fast and clear as the flash and whistle of its breath. *Axe. Axe.* Circles of meaning rippled away from the mark it blazed in the dark of his skull.

Further on a woman emerged from a hut carrying a basket on her hip. She set it down and began pegging clothes on a line, shirts, then trousers, then children's things and a frock. He fingered the rough material of the rag he had kept from the raft – which he wore knotted at his waist, as a sign should he be caught – and had to sit in the tall grass hugging himself, such a rush of bewilderment and soft affection came over him.

He watched the woman hoist the line high by setting a forked pole under it, then pick up her basket and go. The soft things shifted in the breeze. Dripping sunlight, they made gestures this way and that, but awkwardly, weighed down by the shadows in their folds. The hem of a skirt lifted as if lively feet were in movement under it in a shuffling walk.

Later, the same woman came out of her hut and stood making clucking sounds. Is this their language? he thought. He tried it very softly, putting his tongue to the roof of his mouth. *Cluck cluck cluck.*

Suddenly, in a spurt of dust, a mob of big birds shot into sight. All closely bunched and flapping their wings over one another's backs and squawking, they squabbled round the woman's skirt. She laughed, scooped a handful of something from the bowl she carried, tossed it into their midst, then went off again round the side of the hut.

Keeping low to the ground, he scurried forward on all fours, scrabbled among the beaks and claws, and with the maddened birds flying at his arms, and buffeting and pecking, scrambled for cover, then crammed the wet mass into his mouth.

The taste of it, the strangeness, the familiarity, dizzied him. The creature whose dreams he shared came right up to the surface of him. It fed on the saltiness of the stuff, and for a moment entirely took possession of him. He saw things through its eyes in bewildering flashes, and found himself shaken with sobs, but where the tears came from so suddenly, and why, he could not tell. A stranger, a child it might be, who had never wept, was weeping in him. He looked with wonder at his hands and at the remains of the pulpy mess. Wiped it off, a little afraid now of its power, and out of habit muttered syllables that were a formula against bad magic, though he did not think the magic was bad.

He went back to the line where the clothes, brighter now, were filled with sunlight and the lightness of breath. They moved about with vigour and were so lively, so emptily ghostly, that he felt a kind of dread at first of venturing in among them. The shirts made floppy gestures, shook their cuffs, launched out in a gust, and by instinct he ducked. The

31

skirt stirred and swayed. It was like standing in the midst of a crowd that was never still. Now where was that? Where? After a little, with the air ablaze on his shoulders and scents springing up where he trampled the grass, he began to move in and out among them, daring the stroke across his face as he let one soft thing, then another, brush against him, lifting his arms so that a watcher, seeing him pass from one side to the other of the line, dipping his head, might have thought it a kind of dance, a strange blackfeller's dance among the washing. Imagine!

When darkness fell he crept close to the hut. From an opening between the slabs, yellow light poured forth and where it fell made all the sharp little stones of the yard start up in shadow. He stepped round the edge of it, then squatted and very gingerly extended his hand so that the brightness crept up his arm, but there was no warmth to it.

He crept closer and crouched under the sill. From within came voices, and though the words made no sense to him, save for one or two of them, the sound did, the hiss, the buzz.

He put his shoulder to the rough slabs, believing that if he could only get near enough, the meaning of what was said would come clear to him, he would snatch the words clean out of the speakers' mouths. If he could get the words inside him, as he had the soaked mush, the creature, or spirit or whatever it was, would come up to the surface of him and take them. It was the words he had to get hold of. It was the words that would recognise him.

He did not want to be taken back. What he wanted was to be recognised.

So when next day he began to run towards the boundary fence and the paddock where the three children stood staring, he had no notion of abandoning the tribe, even less of breaking from one world to another. It was a question of covering the space between them, of recovering the connection that would put the words back in his mouth, and catch the creature, the spirit or whatever it was, that lived in the dark of him, and came up briefly to torment or tease but could be tempted, he now saw, with what these people ate and with the words they used.

He was running to prove that all that separated him from them was ground that could be covered. He gave no consideration to what might happen when he arrived.

The dog intervened. It flashed out and began snapping at his heels. The boy raised the gun to his shoulder. He sailed up onto the fence rails to save himself, and before he knew it the words were out. The creature or spirit in him had spoken up, having all along had the words in there that would betray him and which, when they came hooting out of his mouth, so astonished him: *Do not shoot. I am a British object.*

It was, after all, the creature, which was so drawn towards them, that had begun to run and for a long moment kept him aloft on the rail, which he gripped with his toes, using his outstretched arms to steady himself, while the dog pranced and slashed the air with its yelping, the boy stood with the gun pointing, clouds rolled, the sky weighed on his neck, and the country, all swamp and forest one way, raw clearings the other, swung in a circle about him.

He waited for a bullet to bring him down, or for the creature, or spirit, to decide it was time to rise upwards and lift him away. But it deserted him, and it was his body that brought him down. On a cry from the smallest of the children, he overbalanced, began to fall, and the next instant was on all fours on the other side.

3

HE WAS TAKEN in by the McIvors, the family of the children who had found him, and given a place to sleep under a red blanket in a lean-to against the side of their hut. In return he helped Jock McIvor round the farm. He was a ready worker, at least to begin with, but could not settle or keep his mind on things; he did not stick, and was physically in too poor a state for the heaviest work. In this respect young Lachlan could run rings around him.

There was, from the beginning, a bond between him and the three children that went back to their meeting at the fence. They felt a proprietary right to him, having seen him first, and he, with his old instinct for self-preservation, for making the most of a weak position, saw the advantage of placing himself in their protection. He let them lead him about like a dog – the dog too took a fancy to him – listened to their secrets, was shown all the bits of things that were precious to them.

He in turn showed them a little of what he knew. He taught the girls to plait grass and make dillybags, to hollow out gourds, dig up the fat yellow or white roots that, once you had thumbed the dirt off, could be baked in the ashes, and to gather berries that yielded a burst of welcome moisture to the tongue or an astringent sweetness.

Making the distinction between them which he had learned among the blacks, he taught Lachlan to track. But the boy anyway stood in a special light for him, and that too went back to the moment of their first meeting, when

Lachlan had stepped out in front of the two girls, raised the 'gun' to his shoulder, and stood there, square and determined, aiming fair at his heart. It had taken him only a moment of course to see that it was just a stick, but that did not mean it was harmless. What it stood for, and the boy's fearful but fearless stance, was more important than stick or gun, and had made an indelible impression on him. He could never look at Lachlan, even if all he was doing was larking about in a childish way, without seeing, in his small compact figure, the power he had laid claim to with the pretence of arms.

His object always was to make himself agreeable to the girls, to play the pupil when they wanted to be teacher, the doll when they wanted someone to dress up. But he kept a watch on Lachlan, ready always if necessary to appease; and the boy, because he was very quick in his perceptions, felt it and knew his power. He led the man on an invisible leash, swaggering before the other children of the place, and only when they were alone together let out his natural affection.

The girls, especially Janet, took a great interest in how he kept himself.

'No, no, Gemmy dear, let *me* do it,' she would say when he failed to button his shirt straight. Or, laughing at the way his hair stuck out in quills and would not be disciplined, 'Sit still, now, there's a good fellow, and I'll brush it and make you neat. I'm giving you a nice parting, Gemmy, see?', and little Meg would hold up the mirror, looking at him rather quizzically over the top of it, while Janet handled the comb.

But there were times, too, when he felt an uneasiness in the older girl, as if she saw that he could not be treated as a child or plaything. He would catch her regard upon him, it was solemn, and an odd feeling would come over him that she was trying to see right into him, to catch his spirit, aware, as the others were not, that he was not entirely what he allowed them to see.

He was surprised. If anyone else had looked at him that way, he would have felt his bowels go soft. But her gaze was so open and vulnerable that he felt no threat in it, and in himself only a stillness, a sense of tender ease at being exposed a moment – not to her, but to himself. Then a cloud would come to her brow and she would glance away.

For her, too, he thought, it was that moment when she had first seen him balanced up there on the fence that she was looking towards, and he felt in the concentration of her gaze that he hung there still. Something, in that moment, had been settled between them, as it had between him and the boy.

He went back and back to it. In the strange flickering light of the empty afternoon, with the sky ablaze on his shoulders, his belly empty, little insects opening and closing their wings over the still grass heads, the long, wavering note of crickets endlessly extended, he would stand gripping the fence rail with his toes, trying to stay up there long enough to take it all in, with the tendency to overbalance growing and growing in his upper body as if it was his heart that had been thrown off balance, and the three children staring: the boy, eyes narrowed, jaw set, with the stick at his shoulder; the dog in midair, also suspended, his tongue dripping; the gawky, fair-haired girl with one hand raised against the sun, the thin wrist arched, and for the first time that puzzled look in her eyes that might, he sometimes felt, just in itself have held him there, never to fall, so intense was the power of her gaze. If he had given himself over to that rather than to the heaviness of his own body, he might have stayed up there for ever. That was what her look meant. Only at that moment he had failed to grasp it.

She was a puzzle to him. He could never be sure what she was thinking. He knew the boy's thoughts because he wanted them known. His power lay in your recognising that he possessed it. It was the power that belonged to him because he was a boy; because, one day, the authority he had claimed in raising the stick to his shoulder would be real. It made him both easier and more dangerous. There was always in your dealings with him something to be taken account of: his concern for those whose eye he was trying to catch. The girl's power was entirely her own. She needed no witness to it.

As for the adults, he soon developed for Ellen McIvor, the mother of the little girls, an affection of a kind he had not known before; he had so little experience in his life of either the domestic or the feminine. It pleased him to find things he could do to make her life easier, and all the more to see the shy, offhand way she accepted them. The desire he had to give her pleasure had in it none of the anxious need to placate that lay behind every gesture he made towards the man of the house. It was free. He felt lightened by it.

Jock McIvor, on the other hand, was from the start uneasy with him. He tried to be fair, to be patient, but his heart was not in it.

When Jock came to him with a request, or more likely a complaint, he felt like running. He shuffled, turned his shoulder; Jock immediately took it the wrong way. 'For God's sake, man, Ah'm no' gonna hit ye. Ah jist want t' tell ye again, ye'd better no' follow the bairns aboot – Ah've telt ye a hunner times. An' ye'd better no' gang wand'rin' on the Mason's side either. Ah've telt ye that as weel. Barney's nervous. Ah dinnae mean t' tell ye again.'

The man was troubled. Gemmy saw it and was watchful. Jock's fear of getting on the wrong side of his friends might in the end be more dangerous to him, he thought, than the open hostility he met in the settlement, where he was always under suspicion, and always, even when no one appeared to be watching, under silent scrutiny.

*

37

What had brought him to them? Even after weeks in which he had become a familiar sight around the settlement, they continued to put the question to one another, or, more darkly, to themselves.

Was he in league with the blacks? As infiltrator, as spy? Did he slip off when they were not watching – they had work to do, they could not always be watching – and make contact with them? Did they visit him secretly at night? Maybe they did not even come in the flesh but had other, less visible ways of meeting and passing information that a white man would not recognise because it was not in a white man's mind to conceive of it. Even those who were well-disposed to the fellow found him unnerving.

He wasn't all there, that's what people said; they meant he was simple. But there were some among them for whom the phrase, light as it was, suggested something darker: that even when he *was* there, in full sunlight, refusing to meet your gaze but engaged, so far as he was capable of it, in conversation, he was halfway gone, across a line, like the horizon, that was not to be fixed in real space, and could begin anywhere.

'He's makin' mugs of yous,' Ned Corcoran asserted. 'You k'n say what you like about 'im. He don't fool me.'

They frowned and looked away.

You learned up here to make allowances, but Ned Corcoran was not a man they had much respect for. His idea of neighbourliness was to send one of his boys across (he had a whole mob of them), usually the soft-eyed eight-year-old, to borrow some implement or other that then found its way into his store. Months later, out of pure generosity, he would lend it out to some other fellow as if it was his own. He'd get it back, too. He'd send the same shamefaced eight-year-old to ask for it, who would stand with his mouth open, breathing, while you fetched it for him. They were indulgent of this little eccentricity but resented it when Ned assumed a superior tone and told them bluntly that the black white-feller was trading on their goodwill.

Was he?

Thwarted by their failure, most of the time, to grasp what the codger was after, and suspecting that his giggling and sidling and hopping about on one foot was meant to make a fool of them, some men would grow hot under the collar and begin to push him about; to the point at times where they had to be restrained. Even those who felt sorry for the man found themselves dismayed by what they called his 'antics'. They felt an urge, when he went into one of his jerking and stammering fits, to look hard at the horizon, and when that yielded no satisfaction, to give grave attention to the dust between their boots. He was a parody of a white man. If you gave him a word for a thing, he could, after a good deal of huffing and blowing, repeat it, but the next time round you had to teach it to him all over again. He was imitation gone wrong, and the mere sight of it put you wrong too, made the whole business somehow foolish and open to doubt.

Poor bugger, he had got lost, and as just a bairn too. It was a duty they owed to what they were, or claimed to be, to bring him back, if it was feasible, to being a white man. But *was* it feasible? He had been with them, quite happily it appeared, for more than half his life: living off the land, learning their lingo and all their secrets, all the *abominations* they went in for. Were they actually looking at a man, a white man, actually putting a knife into his hands and passing him bread, who had –

They broke off, unwilling to let the shadow of it pass their lips and become a fact in their world. If he had, he showed no sign of it, none at all. There was nothing in his snub-nosed, squint-eyed looks and the innocence with which he bit into a crust and went at it with his ground-down,

39

blackened teeth, to show what he might have been privy to in those sixteen years.

He had started out white. No question. When he fell in with the blacks – at thirteen, was it? – he had been like any other child, one of their own for instance. (That was hard to swallow.) But had he remained white?

They looked at their children, even the smallest of them chattering away, entirely at home in their tongue, then heard the mere half-dozen words of English this fellow could cough up, and even those so mismanaged and distorted you could barely guess what he was on about, and you had to put to yourself the harder question. Could you lose it? Not just language, but *it*. *It*.

For the fact was, when you looked at him sometimes he was not white. His skin might be but not his features. The whole cast of his face gave him the look of one of Them. How was that, then?

Mr Frazer had the answer: because his teeth had been worn down almost to the gums from eating the native food. The white man's facial structure came from the different and finer diet. It was the grinding down of his teeth, and the consequent broadening of the jaw that gave him what they called a native look.

Ah, so that was it.

Or – this too came from Mr Frazer and was a harder nut to crack – it was the languages he had learned to speak. He spoke five languages. His jaw, over the years, had adapted itself to the new sounds it had to make. Mightn't it happen after a time that the whole cast of a man's features would be shaped by that, the way a French man, for instance, differs in his whole facial form from an Englishman or a Scot, and so come to share a likeness with the other speakers of the tongue?

Well!

Or both of these, but also the effort he must have made,

in those sixteen years, to blend in and make himself one of them, to find facial expressions, picked up by imitation or reflection and all quite different from a white man's, that would make easier their daily intercourse with him. In taking on, by second nature as it were, this new language of looks and facial gestures, he had lost his white man's appearance, especially for white men who could no longer see what his looks intended, and become in their eyes black.

They chewed on this. Possible. Possible. But were more impressed by something simpler and more disturbing, since it touched on themselves and the sense they had of being in a place that had not yet revealed all its influences upon them.

Wasn't it true (this was not Mr Frazer but another delver into deep things) that white men who stayed too long in China were inclined to develop, after a time, the slanty eyes and flat faces of your yellow man, your Chinese?

Study him, sitting there in the sun with that vacant, in-turned look; heavy-browed, morose. Look at the furrow in his brow. Was it a white man's thought that set it there, or the knowledge of something (they would not name it) that could hardly be conceived of in a white man's thinking, which when the dark recollection of it flickered over his brow, brought it right into the room with you, as a thing you could *smell*. Because for all the scrubbing with raw soap, and the soft woollen shirts and moleskins Ellen McIvor had found for him, and washed with her own hands, he had kept the smell he came with, which was the smell of the myall, half-meat, half-mud, a reminder, a depressing one, of what there might be in him that could not be reclaimed.

His very way of moving was a reminder. He could be in a room before you knew it, his feet scarcely whispering over the hard dirt floor. Your hand would go to the back of your neck as if a fly had lighted there. But there was no fly. You wheeled round and it was *him*, grinning in that foolish apologetic way he had, eager to make up for the shock he

41

had given you by snatching the sopping shirt out of the dirt or fetching water to replace the suds, while you held your side and waited for your heart to return to its place under your ribs.

Of course, it wasn't him you were scared of. He was harmless, or so they said, and so you preferred to believe. It was the thought that next time it might not be him. That when you started and looked up, expecting the silly smile, what would hit you would be the edge of an axe. He made real what till now had been no more than the fearful shape of rumour, though the rumour lately had had a name and number to it: Comet River, nineteen souls.

For at any moment – this was the fact of the matter – they might be overwhelmed. The stoutest of them, stepping out under the stars to take a piss before bed, all unbuttoned and exposed to the night, would feel his balls shrink at the crack of a twig, and tuck himself away without even troubling to shake the last drops off.

Even in broad daylight, to come face to face with one of them, stepping out of nowhere, out of the earth it might be, or a darkness they moved in always like a cloud, was a test of a man's capacity to stay firm on his own two feet when his heart was racing.

It brought you slap up against a terror you thought you had learned, years back, to treat as childish: the Bogey, the Coal Man, Absolute Night. And now here it is, not two yards away, solid and breathing: a thing beside which all you have ever known of darkness, of *visible* darkness, seems but the merest shadow, and all you can summon up to the encounter, out of a lifetime lived on the other, the lighter side of things – shillings and pence, the Lord's Prayer, the half dozen tunes your fingers can pick out on the strings of a fiddle, the names and ages of your children, including the ones in the earth, your wife's touch on your naked belly, and the shy, soft affection you have for yourself – weakens and falls away before the apparition, out of nowhere, of a figure taller perhaps than you are and of a sooty blackness beyond black, utterly still, very close, yet so far off, even at a distance of five feet, that you cannot conceive how it can be here in the same space, the same moment with you.

What you fix your gaze on is the little hard-backed flies that are crawling about in the corner of its bloodshot eyes and hopping down at intervals to drink the sweat of its lip. And the horror it carries to you is not just the smell, in your own sweat, of a half-forgotten swamp-world going back deep in both of you, but that for him, as you meet here face to face in the sun, you and all you stand for have not yet appeared over the horizon of the world, so that after a moment all the wealth of it goes dim in you, then is cancelled altogether, and you meet at last in a terrifying equality that strips the last rags from your soul and leaves you so far out on the edge of yourself that your fear now is that you may never get back.

It was the mixture of monstrous strangeness and unwelcome likeness that made Gemmy Fairley so disturbing to them, since at any moment he could show either one face or the other; as if he were always standing there at one of those meetings, but in his case willingly, and the encounter was an embrace.

4

THE SCHOOLMASTER, George Abbot, let it be thought in the settlement that he was a man of twenty-six or seven with the manners of an older man even than that. He was, in fact, just nineteen, but his plainness, and the severity with which he dealt with every sort of youthful enthusiasm, made possible the deception. He affected a pipe, did not roll his sleeves up, even on days when the heat under the shingles of his one-roomed schoolhouse was at furnace pitch, and when he was invited out on Sundays, did not allow the mothers of his pupils to indulge him with second helpings. He did not wish to be seen as a boy; all the more because he was afflicted with the appetites of one, in a body which, to his consternation, was still growing and which at every point let him down.

In the mean little room they had provided him, behind the blackboard in the room where he extended authority over a rabble of seven to twelve-year-olds, he fought with his loneliness, his youth, and a sensual nature that had been subdued at home by the rigours of convention and the softening presence of his sisters, but also by the duty he felt to his own high prospects. Out here, in the listless air and salt damp of a place where everything was at a point of bursting fullness, he was constantly tormented. All that had once been fine in him had gone to rot, and he had too high a regard for the truth, was too arduous in the exercise of a strict self-scrutiny, not to ask what sort of fineness it might be that was at the mercy of mere conditions and had so easily succumbed.

He knew the falseness of his position and hated it. When he was invited out, he was, often enough, the only one at the table wearing shoes.

The older girls of the household, when they fixed their frank gaze upon him, would make him colour so fiercely that to hide it he had to take the handkerchief from his sleeve and go through the motions of blowing his nose – a performance they regarded as so remarkable that the whole table stopped and stared.

Their brothers, fellows of his own age, sat smirking. They did not know how to address him without doing violence to their own rather shaky dignity. He was Mr Abbot to their parents, and to their little brothers and sisters he was Sir. When he ran into them lounging about the settlement, roughly at ease, as he was not, with their youth, they would fall silent till he passed, then whisper and guffaw, though never loud enough for complaint.

His pupils, thin-cheeked the girls, the boys, some of them almost men, shag-haired and puffy lidded, had been up before dawn to milk cows or do whatever other chores their rough farm life demanded. They swayed at their desks. Their eyelids flickered.

The singing of the nine times table did not enliven them, nor did Shelley's 'To a Skylark' when their young voices sent it out on the torpid air. Defeated by the dullness that glanced back at him from slate-pencil holders gone dark with sweat and the dead blue of their teeth, he felt a slow rage take hold of him.

With an irony of which he was perfectly aware, he chalked up the words from the Reader that they were to learn for homework: *mettlesome, benign, decorum, prudence* ... In the morning, after the monitor had sponged them off, he would hear them over and punish those who got them wrong, the boys and girls equally, one stroke of the ruler for each word misspelled.

A kind of loathing for them, and for himself as well, came with the vinegary odour as they held out their hands, stretched back the fingers and showed the calluses, ragged where they had been picking at them, and the fate-lines grained with dirt.

He hated these petty tyrannies. They mocked with littleness every aspiration he felt towards what was noble and generous in him. But he beat them, and the immediate physical effect was releasing. Then, when he saw the fierce little will with which even the smallest of them clamped their hands in their armpits and fought back tears, he could have burst into tears himself at the shame of it.

He had never meant to come to Australia, least of all to this outlandish part of it.

The only boy in a family of five, he had been educated at the expense of his godfather, a bachelor of luxurious taste and eccentric views who was a distant relation of his mother's, and had once perhaps, or so she liked to suggest, been an admirer. She had no hesitation, when George's father died, in applying to him on the boy's behalf.

Mr Robertson, 'Cousin Alisdair', came to take a look at them, and though, to her disappointment, the great man did not repeat the visit, he did agree to pay for George's schooling, and twice a year, at Easter and Michaelmas, the boy went to stay with him at his country place near Perth. He had presents of pencils and books, and at Christmas little packets of sugar plums and walnuts and sweet-tasting tangerines, which he smuggled home to his sisters; and on his birthday each year was taken to be measured for his suits. The tailor's assistant showed him materials, and advised by Cousin Alisdair he learned to distinguish between the different qualities of tweed, then stood on a box while Mr Davidson, marvelling at how fast he grew, what a sturdy chest he had, applied the tape, and Cousin Alisdair, in a high-backed chair, turned the pages of a magazine.

He was a clever little fellow, with all the pert charm that goes naturally with childish self-assurance, and was soon a favourite with all the servants of the household and its many visitors, who were impressed with the ease with which, in his strapped trousers and tucked shirt, he entered a drawing room, his readiness to answer posers from Cousin Alisdair's legal friends, or to run messages or fetch, with such little-mannish gallantry, a book or a plaid for the ladies, and his ingenuity in devising, out of a stick and the paper from a sweet packet, a swat against the sleepy wasps that came stumbling from the orchard to disturb their rest. He took all this as no more than the tribute due to a charm that was native and irresistible in him, so it was a shock when, at fifteen or so, life dealt him a first and fatal disappointment. The beginnings of a terrible plainness began to declare itself and he saw – it took him a little time to quite grasp it – that people no longer extended the same interest to him, and when he fell back on his old tricks of charm, looked embarrassed: they were no longer appropriate to the big, overgrown fellow he had become.

Cousin Alisdair too lost interest in him. He had offended, he saw, with a good deal of bitterness, against the great man's high regard for the aesthetic. He had to fight hard not to be hurt into a permanent anger at the injustice of things, or become as morose as his heavy looks suggested.

Mr Robertson continued to pay for his upkeep and schooling, and at the beginning of each term to write to him warm, colourless letters, but they no longer met. So it was with a sense of injured pride, and the determination not to show it, that he presented himself, one morning, modestly attired and armed at last with his degree, at George Square to thank his benefactor, as was only proper, for past kindness, but also, he hoped, to receive the offer he had been promised of a place.

The footman who let him in was a well-knit, snub-nosed fellow of his own age, very fancily got up. He was inclined, George thought, to swagger, and as they passed through various rooms and the young fellow stood aside to let him pass, George felt himself the subject of lazy scrutiny, which tempted him to fiddle in a foolish way with his collar.

It was as if this big farm boy, who was, it was true, not a bad-looking fellow, had in conceit at the fine cut of his frock coat, the swelling of his thighs in their pale silk stockings, together with God knows what other articles of smug self-confidence, set up a comparison between them, and settled the thing, with a good deal of satisfaction, in his own favour. George was put off his stride. He had to remind himself, firmly, that he had come here intending to make no appeal to old sentiments, and especially no attempt at old charms. Let his benefactor take him seriously, just as he was.

Mr Robertson was at his desk with the morning mail. George was astonished by how little *he* had changed. He rose up, all freshly scented, lay aside his gold-rimmed spectacles, came round the desk, and embraced George in such warm and unaffected terms that all the resentment he had felt went soft in him and his old eagerness for affection came back in a flood. He had been very fond of Cousin Alisdair at one time.

Mr Robertson retired to the far side of the desk but was all rosy interest.

He was delighted, he really was, to see him so well-grown; to see, too, what good use he had made of himself.

Progress? Excellent. His mother was well? Dear woman. Such happy memories of earlier days. And his sisters?

George was glad of the opportunity this offered to remind Mr Robertson of how they, his mother and sisters, depended on him. Mr Robertson praised his sense of responsibility, he was gratified to see it in so young a man. They were going swimmingly, and moved on easily now to his future. Had he given it any thought? Did he have some idea of what he might do with himself?

Well he had, of course, and in the closeness that had been restored between them, and out of a natural frankness, George took Cousin Alisdair into his confidence in a way he had not originally intended. He put aside the little speech he had prepared and spoke of his feelings, his aspirations, he even ventured a stroke or two of wit; he allowed himself to show off a little, which was forgivable, surely, considering all that was at stake. In the end he made a full confession. Inspired by the usual Sunday school stories, but also by more serious reading among the explorers – and the example, of course, of their own Dr Livingstone – it had come to him, not hastily but after a proper search of his own soul and a great deal of quiet consideration, that his life, his *real* life, lay with the Dark Continent, with Africa. He wanted a life that was arduous; which would call on all his strength – he was physically very strong. He had no idea how Mr Robertson might feel about such things, and he was conscious, always, that he had his mother and sisters to consider and might, for the time being, have to devote himself to something more practical, to trade that is, to business – that was for his benefactor to decide, and of course if it came to that, he would knuckle under, he would be patient – but Africa was where his soul led him, he was certain of this. It was too powerful an idea to be destroyed by the years he might have to devote to moneymaking. He had no illusions about the hardships such a life might present. He was prepared for that. He looked forward to it in fact; work of a kind that would test and stretch and . . .

He was aware suddenly of another voice in the room. Mr Robertson had spoken; two or three syllables that had reached his ear but not as yet his understanding. Carried away by his own enthusiasm he had taken it for granted Mr Robertson would hear him out, and was astonished now to see his benefactor's face, all rosy-cheeked and expectant, lit up by an expression of droll interest and mischievous – could it really be that? – amusement.

Australia. That was the word Mr Robertson had dropped into the room. The silence deepened around it, then spread. Had he, by any chance, Mr Robertson sweetly demanded, his eyes dancing behind circles of thin gold, considered Australia?

Well he had not. Never in his life. Not once. He grew breathless; he tried to keep the great smothering mass of it off.

Australia? He barely knew where it was. He had the uneasy feeling that it had just popped into his benefactor's head. Out of one of those letters perhaps, that by some unhappy coincidence lay in a scatter at his elbow. The arbitrariness of it affected George with a kind of hilarity. The laughter that filled him, and threatened to break out and shatter every object in sight, echoed up from the other side of the world, as Cousin Alisdair, as if eloquent effusion was a family trait, shared even by fifth cousins, began to elaborate, all watered silk but with a glint of steel in his eye, the advantages of that other and rival graveyard – the one George had *not* aspired to. Friends in Sydney . . . Opportunities out there of the highest order . . . Splendid seedground . . . Seven years. (George felt the whole grey mass of it come down upon him.) In the meantime he would see that George's mother was provided for, that his sisters had means to marry, and would be pleased, always, to hear how he was doing . . .

He was doing badly. The seedground, contrary to report, was rank and had been ruinous to him. He thought, and with bitterness, of that swaggering skip-kennel drawing his

50

brows painfully together as he spelled his way through half a column of *The Glasgow Herald*, with no rich godfather to provide for him and no prospects, but, in having the whole town to swagger about in on Sundays, and so many girls to eye and make love to, and clean fingernails and an immaculate shirt, a thousand times more fortunate than he.

Everything that presented itself to his gaze in this godforsaken place told him how mean his life was, how desolate and without hope. Nobody cared for him. He never heard an intelligent word from one day to the next. Africa, he believed, would have tempered his soul to hardness and discovered the man in him. No such demands were made upon him here. The place worked its defeats in a low way. It was on every side oppressive, in all its forms clammy and insidiously sweet – lushness and quick bloom followed by a dank putrescence, so that the soul was at one moment garishly excited, brittle, overwrought, and in the next slothfully laid low. Even the natives were of a dingy greyness. Thin-shanked, dusty, undignified, the life they lived was merely degenerate, so squalid and flea-ridden that it inspired nothing but a kind of horror at what human nature might in its beginnings spring from, and in such a place so easily sink back to.

It was in this light that he considered the yammering, yowling fellow whose story he had taken down that day in his own schoolroom.

He had thought himself very clever then in making his own additions to what he had been set to write down. His fear now was that in following that frivolous urge he had allowed himself to become contaminated, and in the same idle, half-sleepy way in which he did everything here, as if nothing had meaning or consequence.

He forbad the McIvor children to let the fellow accompany them to school, and when his orders were defied – 'We can't help it Sir,' they sang, 'if he just tags along' – took the matter up with the girls' father. The boy, Lachlan, set out deliberately to provoke him. Instead of keeping Gemmy off, he encouraged him and a struggle ensued, of just the little niggling kind that reduced him, in his saner moments, to despair.

He was the brightest of his pupils, this Lachlan Beattie, and might easily have become a favourite; took it for granted, in fact, that he must be. Quick-witted and free in his nature, full of a pert assurance that George recognised only too well, and hungry for praise, he had done everything he could at first to draw attention to himself and win approval; and for this very reason George was determined from the start to deny it. Very deliberately, in a way that the boy was certain to recognise, he ignored him, and Lachlan, perceiving that however quick he was with an answer, however vigorously he waved his hand in the air, he would not be chosen, grew disdainful, then disruptive, then dull. Now, to his usual pointed indifference, George added sarcasm, using the presence of his 'shadow' to mock the boy to his companions. It was Lachlan now who kept Gemmy away.

5

WHEN THEIR MOTHER announced that a cousin was to come out and join them, the two girls were delighted. Kin at last, and a boy! From Scotland, from home. They were to be especially soft with him. His father had been killed in a pit accident, leaving five weans to feed; Lachlan was the eldest.

His father, Rob, had been their mother's favourite among her brothers. When she saw him last he had been a lad of nineteen just newly married. She had made the shirt he was married in out of pure sea-island cotton that cost her two shillings a yard; she had saved a whole six months for it.

They knew all the details of their mother's life at home, she had told it to them a hundred times, but now she told it all again: how her own mother, their grandmother, as a child not much older than they were, had worked down the mine – imagine that now! The house with a little backyard not big enough for a cat to jump in – and here they were with twenty acres. The father and four brothers, all miners. Janet saw them, in her mother's telling, sat down at tea together, still in their pit dirt, black-fisted, noisy, only their eyelids, when they fell to eating, and their teeth when they grinned, showing white in the sooty masks, till one after the other, in the dark little scullery off the yard, they ducked their heads in a tub, soaped their backs and shoulders, and too big now in their whiteness for the low-ceilinged parlour, came towelling their heads and larking about and laughing, and were restored at last – she saw that too – to their separate, recognisable selves: Willie, Ewan, Jamie, Rob.

Her mother as a girl had kept house for them all, washed their shirts, darned their socks, listened to their growls and grumbles, but she hated the pit life and was determined that when she found a man of her own he would never be a miner. She had watched them grow up, each one, from eager, affectionate little lads into coarse fellows who pushed down and extinguished everything that was fine in them. On Saturday nights they were no better than any other of the Airdrie men. They got into fights, came home bruised but elated, then lay stupefied.

When their daddie turned up – Janet, glancing up, saw him grin, very pleased with himself and looking twenty years younger – it was just in time, she told them. She was already twenty-four and on the way to being an old maid. One of her brothers brought him in after a football game, but she had seen him already in a tug of war team the summer before. A big, raw-boned, fair-skinned, sandy fellow. Silly drunk and a bit ashamed of himself, he was still as a stockfish on that first occasion, though he was bold enough later. He worked as a gardener, like his father, on a big estate. Her brothers warned her, teasingly, that he wasn't as tame as he looked, that he liked a dram, had an eye for the girls; but she had seen that for herself. She wasn't put off.

Janet listened to all this in a kind of dream, as she always did when her mother spoke of things that brought the world back there alive in her; she clung to every detail, she couldn't get enough of it. She was in love with this other life her parents had lived; with Scotland and a time before they came to Australia, before she was born, that was her time too, extending her life back beyond the few years she could actually recall, and giving reality to a world she had need of; more alive and interesting, more crowded with *things*, with people too, than the one she was in. This cousin who was coming would bring some of that with him. He would still have its light upon him, alive and actual. He would have its speech in his mouth.

But when he arrived he showed no gratitude for the chance they were offering him, and wasn't at all pleased to see them. He was a stocky, tough lad of nine, a town boy. Airdrie, he told them loftily, was a *toon*. The bush – it wasn't even country – was of no interest to him, and Janet saw, because he set out in his superior know-all way to make her see it, that the things they had been saving to show him, all their little treasures and secrets, were in his eyes poor – she had not seen till now just how poor. She felt humiliated, as if the poverty was in them. It did not occur to her that he might be protecting himself; that his refusal to enter into their world might be a fear of losing, more than he had done already, the one he had left and was heartsick for. He scoffed and swaggered. Nothing here was good enough for him.

He began every sentence with 'At hame in Scotland' – yet at home, as she knew from her mother, they had been starving. She would harden her heart and mock him. 'Oh, at hame in Scotland,' she would sing, imitating his accent, which she also loved. He went red in the face and could barely hide his tears.

She had her triumph. But seeing it she felt ashamed, it was so easy. And Scotland, home, was sacred to her. She was going against herself when she mocked it.

There were times when she felt helpless against a place which, as her parents evoked it in every word they uttered, belonged so much more strongly to all the highest emotions in her than the place she was in. And he had seen it, and she had not. He would have that over her forever.

After a time he discovered what he was endowed with that gave him an advantage over her and used it mercilessly; except that the thing was so native, so accidental in him, that though he could name it, even he did not know what

it really was. He was full of scorn when she failed to understand some word he used, and took delight, with their
mother, in slipping into the old tongue. He would look
towards her with his eyes wide and innocent but a little smile
of satisfaction on his mouth that for the moment he had
shut her out. Her fist ached to wipe the smug look from his
face, and he knew it, and was more cocky than ever. 'I don't
understand,' little Meg would whine. 'What's splairgin'?
What's a moothfu' o' mools?' But *she* would not ask.

The struggle between them was fierce. Till Lachlan came
she had been used to going her own way, unconditioned and
free. She had no limit to herself. Now she resented his easy
assumption that he was superior, should take the lead in all
their doings, and that she must naturally yield to him.

She was half a head taller, for the moment she had that
over him; but it would not last, she had no illusions about
that. (She had long ago discovered the satisfaction of tor-
menting herself with hard truths.) She sought out ways to
hurt him. He was very proud and liked to believe he was
tough, but he cried easily, she could make him cry. Then,
when she did, she was shocked, felt miserable, and longed,
against her own interest, to comfort him, though she saw
that if she did he would hate her for it.

Sometimes for a day or two they would be close. Full of
liveliness and schemes for fresh adventure, he was easy so
long as you gave in to him. He had always to assert himself
and be first. He was in love with his own nobility but at the
same time needed to boast, and of things, Janet saw, that
were not always true. It offended her own sense of inviolable
honesty. She was hard on herself; why should she be less
hard with him? She was consumed after a time with the need
to expose him, to make him confess that so much of what
he claimed was just another attempt to intimidate and assert
himself and the superiority of 'hame'; which might be true

56

– the latter in fact *was* true – but she could not let him be the judge of it.

She would have forgiven him all if he had shown any sign of humbling himself. She was full of affection, she wanted to love him, and longed for some softening in him that would allow it without loss of pride. But first he had to admit need, and he would not. Everything she and Meg knew, and he did not, was not worth the knowing.

They showed him the reddish-gold resin that ironbarks wept, which when you chewed it had a bitter flavour. He spat it out and thought they were making a fool of him.

They showed him bacon-and-eggs bushes. He told them scornfully, 'That's no' them. That's no' the *real* wans.' He had seen bluebells. When he stood up and sang of them in his high clear voice, Janet was overwhelmed and their mother wept. He glowed. He was radiant. The light of some far-off place she had only imagined shone through his skin.

She slipped away and stared into a glass but could find no such beauty – no promise of it either – in herself. She was gangly and freckled. She had warts on her hands. And there was such a hunger for beauty in her. The appearance of it in Lachlan did not make her envious. It struck her with awe, as of something impersonal, that commanded her absolutely beyond her will.

But he saw after a time, for all his stubbornness and pride, that if he was to get on here he would have to know the place. He set out, in a dogged way, to learn all the little skills and tricks of bushcraft, and because he was quick and had to be first in everything was soon as much a bushman as the best of them, with a grit, and a fierce little-mannish tenacity that even Jim Sweetman grew to respect. Jock McIvor was proud of him. They tracked and hunted together, shot scrub turkey, and bronze-wings and topknots and fruit pigeon, and in the ti-tree forest on the margin of the lagoons a dozen varieties of duck.

It was a flame in the boy, this power he had acquired over the world they moved in. He gave up being contemptuous, since he was the one now who 'knew things', assumed an easy, masculine air that he had picked up by imitation from his elders, and was so good at it that it looked like nature. And what of me? she thought. I am as brave as he is. I could do all that. Being in possession now of so many skills, and the code that went with them and belonged to men, he had put himself beyond reach. And she was still, if only by an inch now, the taller!

She resented bitterly the provision his being a boy had made for him to exert himself and act. He had no need to fret or bother himself; only to be patient and let himself grow and fill out the lines of what had been laid up for him. The assurance of that, and of his own will, gave him a glow you might never have guessed at from the thin-faced, thin-shouldered town lad he had been when he first came to them. He would grow quickly now. The vision of what lay before him would square his shoulders, deepen his voice, give him room.

She had no such vision of her own future. All she saw laid up for herself was what her mother presented, a tough pride in competence, in being unflagging and making no fuss. She admired her mother but the narrowness of it was terrible to her.

All silent mutiny, she would stand punching at a lump of dough at her mother's table, and might have gone on doing it forever – stood there with one bare foot on the other on the dirt floor, punching away at her own dull lump of a soul. Her mother watched and was concerned. She looked up and smiled, a wan attempt. Her mother was not fooled.

She pored over books, anything she could lay her hands on that offered some promise that the world was larger, more passionate, crueller – even that would be a comfort – than the one she was bound to.

She sat over a piece of simple needlework, and worked as if her life was in every stitch; as if one day the angel of the Last Judgment would hold up the pot-holder with its design of forget-me-nots, point to a stitch that was too small, or not straight, and say for the whole world, all the gathered souls of all the ages to hear: 'Janet McIvor, did you do this?'

One day, hunched in the shade of a scrubby lemon tree, picking idly at a scab on her knee, she was amazed, when the hard crust lifted, to discover a colour she had never seen before, and another skin, lustrous as pearl. A delicate pink, it might have belonged to some other creature altogether, and the thought came to her that if all the rough skin of her present self crusted and came off, what would be revealed, shining in sunlight, was this finer being that had somehow been covered up in her.

When she got up and walked out into the paddock, and all the velvety grass heads blazed up, haloed with gold, she felt, under the influence of her secret skin, suddenly floaty, as if she had been relieved of the weight of her own life, and the brighter being in her was very gently stirring and shifting its wings.

In a particular vibrancy of light that on another occasion might have given her a headache, all the world shimmered and was changed.

The paddock of standing wheat when she wandered out into it boomed with a flaminess that bounced and struck out flares, then was quenched by a passing cloud.

Grasshoppers, pinches of dust but with spring-like muscles in their thighs that allowed them to leap distances that in human terms would have been hundreds of yards, seemed made of the finest glass, and she too felt fine-spun, toughly transparent.

Trees shook out ribbons of tattered bark, and the smooth skin under it was palest green, streaked orange like a sunset, or it had the powdery redness of blood. *Glory* was the word she thought of. A part of her rose into vague, bright zones where her name, she thought, ought to have been Flora; she hated plain Janet. In giving it to her they had set her too low and thus too early settled her fate. (It was Flora Macdonald she had in mind, but some other dream-figure with flowers round her hem and bright petals opening miraculously out of the clods at her feet might also have been there in the regions she moved in an inch or two above the earth.)

But she was a practical child and sceptical of mere feelings. They blazed up a moment, then died and left you stranded, barefoot, in the grass. She did not put too much store by them, but they were important enough, these moments, for her to keep them to herself.

Unlike Lachlan. When he was fired up with something he had to let it out. That was what made things difficult for him. Full of bright schemes for the future, heroic visions in which the limitations of mere boyhood would at last be transcended, he felt that if he could only see them clearly enough they would be there, up ahead, waiting for him to catch up bearing the details at last of place and time.

As soon as he was old enough, with Gemmy as his guide, he would get up an expedition to search for Dr Leichhardt. Somewhere along the way he might be wounded by blacks. Gemmy would nurse him back to health with herbs only the natives knew of. He would discover two or three rivers, which he would name after some of his acquaintances, and a mountain to which he might give his aunt's name, Mount Ellen, or the name of some place in Scotland, and they would find Leichhardt, or his bones at least, and when they got back and people wanted to put up a monument, he would insist, nobly, that Gemmy's name should be inscribed there along with his own. Then, when all that was done . . .

There was no end, no limit either, to his plans.

Janet could not take it seriously, not because she did not believe in his capacity, one day, to do such things, but because the things themselves were so ordinary. Her view was that when real life caught up with you, it would not be in a form you had already imagined and got the better of. But she had no wish any longer to bring him down, so in this too he had his triumph over her.

The chief sharer of his visions was Gemmy, who listened, grasped only half of what he heard, and made his own assessments.

What moved him most was to see that he too was there in the boy's dreams. He felt a rush of affection at being trusted and given a place in what Lachlan Beattie had laid up to himself, but also a fearful protectiveness that Lachlan, if he had perceived it, would have resented.

He was just a child! The realisation shocked Gemmy but settled him too. It was not often here that he could reclaim a sense of himself as a grown man.

6

From the beginning there were those among them, Ned Corcoran was the most vehement, for whom the only way of dealing with blacks was the one that had been given scope elsewhere. 'We ought to go out,' he insisted, controlling the spit that flooded his mouth, 'and get rid of 'em, once and for all. If I catch one of the buggers round my place, I'll fuckin' pot 'im.' He jerked out the last couple of syllables, and the explosion they made, and the silence afterwards, made some men uncomfortably hot. The rest shifted their boots but did not speak. They were not so candid as Ned Corcoran, but did not essentially disagree with him. It was the quickest way; the kindest too maybe, in the long run. They had seen what happened to blacks in places where the locals were kind. It wasn't a pleasant sight.

But there were others, the milder members of the settlement, who argued that it was surely worth trying a softer policy. What they looked forward to was a settled space in which they could get on with the hard task of founding a home, and maybe, if they were lucky, a town where in time all the civilities would prevail. If they got the preliminaries right, the natives too might be drawn in, as labourers, or house-servants. They had secretly, some of them, a vision of plantations with black figures moving in rows down a field, a compound with neat whitewashed huts, a hallway, all polished wood, with an old grey-haired black saying 'Yessir', and preparing to pull off their boots (all this off in the future of course, maybe far off; for the moment they would not mention the boots since most of them did not have any). They ought at least, so they thought, to use this Gemmy fellow to get some reliable information that would temper with fact the fantastic rumours that flew about the place and kept them in a state of permanent anxiety. What haunted them was the endless round of reprisals they would be involved in if one of their number got jumped and speared (as God knows could happen easily enough) and some hothead like Ned Corcoran took it into his head to get up an extermination party.

So from the beginning his questioners, Gemmy saw, were of two kinds.

One lot wanted to make an ally of him in what they hoped would be an easy war.

They were affable, these fellows. They offered him chews of tobacco, squatted on their heels, and hummed and harred and looked off into the distance – he had a good idea what they were seeing there. They fished about, first one, then another, in a casual way, for what they wanted to know: whether the tribes, out there, up there, were in the habit of gathering at any one particular spot, and in what numbers, and if it was just the men or the whole mob of them, women and children as well. They chewed their tobacco and shot out the juice, or quietly smoked, with no urgency in them; but he felt the purpose in their hands, saw in their eyes the volleys of grey smoke spreading, then hanging like rain. They chuckled to themselves and thought he could not hear. He chewed his tobacco and was still.

When he first came among them he had been unable to tell from their wooden expressions, and the even more wooden gestures, what they had in their heads. They hid what they felt as if they were ashamed of it, or so he had decided; though whether in front of others or before themselves, he could not tell. Their eyes, their mouths, seemed dead in the rigid faces. Only slowly, after long watching, did he begin to distinguish the small signs that made them trackable: the ball of gristle in the corner of a man's cheek, which you could actually hear the soft click of if you listened for it; the swelling of the wormlike vein in a man's temple just below the hairline, the tightening of the crow's feet round his eyes, the almost imperceptible flicker of pinkish, naked lids; a deepening of the hollow above a man's collarbone as his throat muscles tensed, and some word he was holding back, because it was unspeakable, went up and down there, a lump of something he could neither swallow nor cough up. He saw these things now, and what astonished him was how much they gave away. Perhaps their faces were more expressive because he could catch these days more of the words they used, even the ones they left unspoken. So long as he was deaf to the one he had been blind to the other. No more.

So he hummed and harred and chewed his tobacco, and when he was forced to speak at last, put them off with answers which, by shifting a landmark and counting a few dead in with the living, set his people further north than they actually were and made them more numerous. He felt a heavy responsibility.

They were sly. They pretended to be pleased with him. He too was sly, but was less sure than he would have liked to be that he had told them nothing they might use. He leapt about, and with his heart very heavy in him, joked a little, and they narrowed their eyes, all smiles. 'Good boy, Gemmy,' Ned Corcoran said, as if he could have brained him.

But it was the other lot, those who were looking for the soft way, who gave him trouble. They could not understand why he was holding out on them. They were the peaceable ones, the ones who wanted to avoid bloodshed, couldn't he see that? Couldn't he tell the difference? Urgency made them desperate. They shouted at him, and then at one another.

And in fact a good deal of what they were after he could not have told, even if he had wanted to, for the simple reason that there were no words for it in their tongue; yet when, as sometimes happened, he fell back on the native word, the only one that could express it, their eyes went hard, as if the mere existence of a language they did not know was a provocation, a way of making them helpless. He did not intend it that way, but he too saw that it might be true. There was no way of existing in this land, or of making your way through it, unless you took into yourself, discovered on your breath, the sounds that linked up all the various parts of it and made them one. Without that you were blind, you were deaf, as he had been, at first, in their world. You blundered about seeing holes where in fact strong spirits were at work that had to be placated, and if you knew how to call them up, could be helpful. Half of what ought to have been bright and full of the breath of life to you was shrouded in mist.

So they shouted at him in one language and he clenched his teeth on another, and the angrier they grew, the more he saw that it was better to keep to himself what even the good men among them were trying to rattle out of him.

There was an exception to this, an odd one.

He ought to have been intimidated by Mr Frazer, the minister – most of the others were; it had not escaped him that even the loudest among them went tongue-tied when the minister approached, though they were quick to reclaim their prestige as hard fellows by scoffing at the man as soon as he was gone. But Gemmy, from that first day at the schoolhouse, had attributed to Mr Frazer a gift of understanding which somehow saw right through to what he wanted to express, and often enough, before he himself knew it. He trusted the minister, and was happy in his presence to open himself entirely to whatever might emerge from their silent communing when, in the cool early mornings, and sometimes again in the late afternoon, they went out together to *botanise*, as Mr Frazer called it, in the scrub country on the far side of the creek, or along the shady gallery of the creek itself where it climbed the escarpment to the west.

Mr Frazer on these outings wore a wide-awake hat, much frayed at the edges, and bore on a strap over his shoulder a portable inkstand, and in another bag, of canvas, a set of fat little books. Here, to Gemmy's delight, he sketched the parts of the plants Gemmy showed him, roots, leaves, blossoms, with straight little arrows in flight towards them from one side or other of the page, where Mr Frazer, in his careful hand, after a good deal of trying this sound and that, wrote the names he provided.

It disturbed him at first, it offended his sense of propriety, that what Mr Frazer wanted to see were the same things he showed the McIvor girls: women's business. What would the other men think if they knew of it? He felt ashamed for the man, but lost his concern at last in the sheer joy of being free again to wander, and in the satisfaction he felt at the co-operation between them that made him the hands and eyes of the enterprise, the breath too when it came to giving things a name, as Mr Frazer was the agency for translating it out of that dimension, which was all effort, sweat and dirt, and grubbing with your nails, and thorns, and scratches, into these outlines on the page that were all pure spirit, the product of stillness and silent concentration.

It was always the same routine. He named the fruit as he plucked it, biting into the flesh or splitting it (the fig or apple as Mr Frazer called them) to show the pulp, or, if it was a berry, staining his mouth with its juice. Then he passed the thing to Mr Frazer, who sniffed, then warily, his mouth screwed up like an arsehole, tasted, and gave a smile as he savoured, or yowled and spat. Then he too tried the name on his tongue; took, as Gemmy saw it, a preliminary lick at the yam or tuber to reveal a streak of colour or test the

66

roughness of its skin, as he himself had done, more vigorously, with his thumb. He did not often get it right. He did not open his mouth wide enough, or his tongue was in the wrong place or lolled about like a parrot's, or he put too much spit into the thing or too little. Gemmy was glad that none of the clan were there to hear it.

To get a name wrong was comic but could also be blasphemous. In one case what emerged from Mr Frazer's mouth was an old man's testicle, in another, the tuber came out as a turd. Of course he understood immediately that he had botched the thing and after a good deal of trying amended it, but so scandalously on one occasion that Gemmy was shocked, and looked about fearfully, since the word Mr Frazer had hit upon was one the surrounding spirits should never have heard on a *man's* lips, and he worried a little that some of these things might get into the book.

He was sensitive to this dealing between name and spirit. It was out of a kind of reverence, as well as concern for the danger he might put them in, that he concealed from Mr Frazer, who he knew would not notice, a good deal of what he himself could see. Things it was forbidden them to touch, since they were in the care of the men whose land they were crossing; others that only women could approach; others again that were a source of more power than he could control. They could have nothing to do with these things without creating a disturbance in the world that would do him, and Mr Frazer, and others too perhaps, irreparable injury.

So when he and the minister, half-crouching, pushed in under the overhanging boughs of a gully or trudged up a rocky, sun-scorched slope to where they could see, north and west, all the country he was at home in, he was moving through a world that was alive for him and dazzling; some of it even in the deepest shade throwing off luminous flares, so that he had to squint and cover his eyes, and all of it crackling and creaking and swelling and bursting with growth; but he cast the light only in patches for Mr Frazer, leaving the rest undisclosed.

Once or twice on these outings he saw blacks who were unfamiliar to him standing frozen in the brush, every muscle alert.

He made no obvious sign to them, none anyway that Mr Frazer would observe, since he knew the suspicions the white men had of him; but very gravely, in passing, acknowledged the watcher's claim, and they accepted and let them pass.

On other occasions he saw nothing but felt the presence of watchers as a coldness at the base of his spine, a thickening of the darkness to one side of the track. Once again, he acknowledged them, whether they were there or not.

Mr Frazer saw nothing at all. Even when they were meant to be seen, he did not distinguish them from the surrounding vegetation or the play of light and shadow between the leaves. Puffing and singing odd little songs to himself, and fanning away flies, and calling Gemmy to notice this or that, he went barging through; and Gemmy did not enlighten him.

As for what the blacks would be seeing, Gemmy knew what that was. He himself would have a clear light around him like the line that contained Mr Frazer's drawings. It came from the energy set off where his spirit touched the spirits he was moving through.

All they would see of Mr Frazer was what the land itself saw: a shape, thin, featureless, that interposed itself a moment, like a mist or cloud, before the land blazed out in its full strength again and the shadow was gone, as if, in the long history of the place, it was too slight to endure, or had never been.

7

'Oh, I wouldna' concern yursel wi' Gemmy. He's
hairmless.'

This was Jock McIvor to the little group of neighbours
that on odd days gathered where three farms came together
high on a slope; not by arrangement, it was never formal,
but by an unspoken agreement that it was the sort of evening,
at the end of a hard day, when a man might take a stroll
uphill, have a smoke and see what was doing; in the harshness of their lives up here a point of easy fellowship and
repose. He was making reply to a doubt his neighbour,
Barney Mason, had expressed. It wasn't a complaint – the
code of friendship between them forbad that; rather, a long-
standing anxiety on Barney's part that was general but had
recently, to Jock's distress, found its focus in the white black
man.

Gemmy had been with them for five months but Jock had
not got used to him. When he had agreed that first afternoon
to take the fellow in – in the confused excitement of the
occasion, with the children noisily clamouring and his wife
making silent appeal that just this once he might relax his
strictness and indulge them – he had been acting against his
own better judgment. He knew that and had gone right on
and let the thing happen. He had done it out of embarrassment; because he did not want exposed before others a
difference between Ellen and himself that was private, and
which he felt she ought not to take advantage of.

He did offer a protest but it was a weak one. Their life

was hard enough already; did they need a new addition to the household? 'But Jock,' she said quietly, 'look at the puir creature! He'll be nae trouble – Lachlan'll see t' him.'

He had made no further argument because the chief thing he had against the man was so unreasonable; he was ashamed of it.

From the moment he saw the fellow he had felt a kind of repulsion, a moral one he thought, though it expressed itself physically. Even now when he was used to having him about the place, and saw what a pathetic creature he was – how keen to make himself useful and how good with the children – he could not get past what he had felt on the first day, and so far as he could recall, at the very first sight of him hobbling down the gully with Lachlan driving him. He could not bear to have Gemmy come close to him. If he did, and tried to touch him, out of gratitude it might be for some small kindness, for he was very emotional, he would lose his head. 'There's nae ca' for that, man – enough! For God's sake, get off o' me!' Gemmy would look baffled. It was Ellen who had to step in and restore things. 'A'richt, Gemmy, that's enough, there's a guid lad. Just step ootside, will ye, and fetch me an armful o' wuid.'

So when he put Barney off with an assurance of Gemmy's harmlessness he was being truthful in one way – there was no physical harm in him – but in a deeper way he was not.

He was a worrier, Barney. He was forever gowling or greeting over one thing and the next. Though not much more than thirty, he wore a permanent dent in his brow, as if someone, years back, or some *thing* more likely, had let him have it with a slingshot; though it was also possible that the blow was still to come. Jock sympathised but had decided he could do most good by making light of Barney's fears while admitting, secretly, they might be real.

Worrying out loud was Barney's way of dealing with things. His own way was to clamp down hard and keep his troubles to himself. He wasn't sure it was more effective than Barney's, but it suited him. When Barney developed this bee in his bonnet about Gemmy he did not know how to save himself. He hated the difference it made between them, the looks of appeal Barney cast at him, and uncomprehending disappointment; even more that the constraint between them should be revealed when others were about. It was a shame. It spoiled things.

Under the hard conditions of life up here neighbours were important, and over the last years he and Barney had become more than that. Their huts were visible, one from the other, through the half-cleared forest – or at least the lights were. Polly Mason was Ellen's best friend. The children, when they had no chores to do, went off together on adventures in the scrub, swapped treasures, had quarrels that kept them apart for a day or two but were soon patched up. They had never worried about fences or boundaries. So when they took Gemmy on, the Masons too were affected, and Barney did not like it. Gemmy was warned against straying across on to the Masons' land, and so far as Jock knew, complied, but Barney, in his anxious way, was forever out there pacing the line and looking for signs of trespass; except that there was no line, and the trespass too might be no more than a shadow on Barney's thoughts, and how could you deal with *that*? All he could do was meet the ritual complaint with ritual reassurance, and hope that conversation, which was slow up here, with many pauses that easily took the place of words, would have moved on under their long-drawn silence and when it resurfaced hit a new topic. But on this occasion he had no luck.

'Yair well,' Ned Corcoran put in after a longish gap, 'I dunno about that. You'd be the best judge a' that, Jock, you an' Barney. How harmless the cove is. Seein' yer all so close. On'y I woudn' want 'im hangin' roun' *my* place. Coudn' sleep at night – I k'n hardly sleep now. I'd be askin' meself

– you know – if 'e wasn' – you know – receivin' visits. From ol' frien's.'

They shifted their boots in the dust. Jock's heart fell. And Hec Gosper, the youth whose hammer Gemmy had wrestled for that first day, and who ever since had harboured a kind of grudge, dropped his chin to conceal a smile.

He was new among them, having just moved up from the group of half-grown boys who hung about the verandah of the store. He did not say much, he was still on trial here, but he was very observant. He had recently discovered in himself a streak of irony that he found scope for in the play that went on under the slow utterances of these fellows, but even more in the depth of their silences. It amused him, for instance, that they had begun to regard Jock McIvor, who was one of the little inner band, with a closer eye; as if he had developed a mark of difference, or some deformity had emerged in him that they had failed till now to observe.

What intrigued Hector was that Jock McIvor, who had always been such an acceptable bloke, with all the easy confidence a man derives from it, had begun to lose that magic quality. Little defensive spikes and spurs appeared in him that surprised the others and increased a suspicion that they might somehow have been mistaken in him.

Hector owed his expertise in these matters to his lip, though it otherwise offered no impediment to his view of himself (and especially since it had begun to be obscured with the softness of a moustache) as a flash young fellow and potential dandy, if he could only get away to Brisbane, or any place in fact with barbershops, pool rooms, buggies in the street, and of an evening the glow of streetlamps and the clicking on the pavement of women's heels. He saw himself in tall boots with a yard of ribbon behind his hat, but stood meanwhile, barefooted and with his head down, stroking the hair on his lip, while Ned Corcoran, who was persistent, led them back to where they had stuck.

'Yair, well,' he said, 'it's the wife I'd be worried about. If it was me. You know what I mean? Gracie.'

There, Hec thought, Jock McIvor. What now, eh?

He had no malice towards Jock. Malice was not in his nature. It was the spectacle itself that drew him, the discovery, which was new, that there might be more in the world to dwell on than just himself.

Jock swallowed hard. He restrained himself from replying that Gracie Corcoran, unlike his own wife, was a mouse, if not a bandicoot. But it saddened him, all this. He felt the knot in his throat as a hard little nut of injustice. That the others did not come to his aid – Jim Sweetman for instance, who merely looked embarrassed and turned away. That Ned Corcoran, a man for whom they had no respect, should be glancing about now with such cocky assurance that he had hit the mark and was being listened to.

None of what followed was new, though it wounded him just the same; they were not original, these fellows. What surprised Jock was that not so long ago he would not have seen it, and if he had would have found reassurance in their being so easily predictable. He had begun lately to be critical, even of Jim Sweetman, and he did not want to be. He did not like the experience, which was new, of seeing his friends from a distance, of finding them on one side and himself on the other, and the knowledge that if he was seeing them with new eyes, he too, since the distance must work both ways, had become an object of scrutiny. He was disturbed, most of all, by the view this gave him of *himself*. As if there was something in him that justified scrutiny. That he might be less open than he appeared.

Watching Jock's difficulty with Gemmy, the terror, which was almost comic, into which he was thrown by the poor fellow's extravagant bursts of feeling, Ellen McIvor found

73

herself taken back to a vision of Jock that had been obscured in these last years by the hardships they had been through. She had been attracted then by a quality in him that went oddly with his big frame, and must, she thought, be what other women too were drawn to, a mixture of forcefulness and almost girlish modesty.

Work in the outdoors had burnished him; he was ruddy. His flesh, when his sleeves were rolled, had none of the dead marble whiteness she knew from her brothers and associated with the sunless world underground. It glowed. You felt the heat of it right through his shirt. It carried a scent of grass and clean sunlight she had longed for all her life, or so she believed, in the dismal world she had grown up in, where everything was smudged and smirched with coal dust and even the air you breathed was gritty, and the taste in your throat always of tar.

He had wanted them to go to Canada. That was what he offered, along with himself. But when they got down to it, Australia seemed the larger choice. There was land there and sunlight (she could not wait) and spaces, he told her, they could barely conceive of here. But *she* could. Sunlight and space were the first things she had glimpsed in him.

They arrived in Brisbane in a January swelter. The town, its muddy streets made passable by duckboards, its houses, huts rather, mere makeshift affairs of bark and iron among dark, glossy-leaved figs, was a low place, sunk in a steamy torpor where everything the flesh touched was damp and the flesh itself damper, and the air had a sweetish smell just this side of putrescence. The drunkenness they met in the streets had a desperation to it that made her wonder what there might be in the place, given so much space, that could madden the men and made the women so pinched and colourless. It was not what they had expected. Jock turned gloomy, and she saw for the first time then that the sunniness she had seen in him was not his real nature. She was the one who had to insist that the heat was not too bad, or the steamy rain when it gushed down, or the clouds of mosquitos that blew in from the mangrove-choked islands in the river's mouth, and whose bites made his eyelids swell; or the cockroaches, big as wrens, that came flying in at every open window and ran over their faces in the dark; or the delays. A different kind of balance was established between them in these first days in the colony, as if, in coming halfway round the world, they had arrived not so much at a new place as a new accommodation with their own natures.

The delays went on, their money dwindled; they had to take cheaper lodgings where they were separated into dormitories, male and female, and still there was no sign of the land they had been promised. At last, when it was clear that they could expect nothing of others and must act for themselves, they left Brisbane for the Darling Downs, he to work as a general hand on a big holding, she as a housemaid. And Jock, in his disappointment, his shame too, perhaps, at having promised her so much and provided so little, began to refine in himself the stringy, hard-bitten qualities of dourness and harsh self-discipline that the land itself appeared to demand, and which, for all the fierceness of its own sunlight, dashed out the last of sunniness in him. She had Janet, then lost a little boy, then a girl. They stuck it out, saved what they could, and when land was opened in the unsettled districts beyond the Burdekin, came north. She had left more of herself than she dared consider in the rooms of the homestead whose wide verandahs she had scrubbed and in the copper where week after week, on Mondays, she had boiled the household wash; most of all in the two small graves she knew she would not see again, under the black soil in the grove of bunyas.

Jock, harder than ever now, since more was at stake, dealt sternly with himself and with the children too, Meg when she came, then Lachlan. She saw the last of his youth burned out of him in the hot, bushfire summers up here, when the whole sky, for days on end, was a glowing furnace. And it was to recall a little of his old light-hearted gallantry then – for her own sake, as well as his – that she would tease him about the girls she had won him away from; she knew their names from her brothers – Annie McDowell, Lettie Davidson, Minnie Kyle – happy to see, for all his protests, that it pleased him, woke some spark of his old shy devilry in him, to be taken back to his youthful conquests and the fair lad who had had to dip his head, that first time, silly-drunk as he was, at the door of their parlour. In time this teasing became a show to amuse the two little girls, but also to give them a glimpse of some other side of their stern father. They loved to hear the names – there were so few names in their lives.

'What was she like,' they would insist, 'Lettie Davidson? Tell about Lettie.'

'Oh, ye'll hae t'ask yer faither aboot that,' she would tell them. 'Ah never clapt eyes on the huzzie. Tell them, Jock.'

He looked foolish. 'Get awa' wi' ye, thir wasnae ithers,' he told her.

'Keep me!' she'd laugh. 'Sic lees the man tells. Look at the colour of him. Look at yer faither and see what lees a man can tell.' It relieved him.

He was often homesick though he did not say so. The land here never slept. If only he could wake one day and find it, just for a day, under a blanket of snow! What he missed were the marks of change. The crying, high up, of curlews flocking to a new season, to some place thousands of miles to the north where it had been winter and was now breathing the freshness of spring, brought an ache to his heart for the sight of rowans just bursting into sticky leaf, and for days afterwards he would be rough-tempered, as if the need of bark for the shiver of radiance was in himself.

She could not afford such surrenders. Her nature was

less volatile than his, less prone to extremes. Occasionally, washing an old frock with a pattern of larkspurs, all their lively colour gone to grey, she would experience a little pang at the thought that she might never again see one. She had chosen the print, years ago, because she had loved so much their vivid blue. But she had few regrets for the world she had left – perhaps because she had none at all for her youth. She lived in the demands of the moment, in the girls, in Lachlan, and was too high-spirited, too independent, to care whether other women approved of her.

They came in the afternoon with their bits of darning. As the needles went in, they lowered their eyes and put their questions, all barbed concern.

Gemmy, it was always Gemmy. What had they talked of, she wondered, before Gemmy arrived to give that breathless urgency to their talk and to darken the air in the close little hut to a point where she wondered, sometimes, how even by screwing their eyes up they could find the hole to thread a needle, the room was so dense with the shadows they called up to terrify themselves and one another.

Didn't she find it hard sometimes to sit at the same table with him? Considering that he might be happier running about naked – goodness, remember that first day! – than in the shirts she washed for him. Oh and the trousers, of course! And eating grubs – imagine! – than potatoes and cold mutton. That is, if it wasn't something worse. Their own grandfathers, so they say. And wasn't she scared, just a little – well they knew *she* wasn't but they would be, it was a wonder really how calm she was – of the time he spent with the children. The little girls, for instance. And Lachlan, who was so lively and impressionable? Wasn't she worried sometimes about the influence the fellow might be having? And did she really let him chop wood for her? Actually let him loose with an *axe*?

The word assumed substance, took shape, and you heard

the swish of its blade through the stilled air in the suspension of their breath. Gracie Corcoran, who was a Roman, crossed herself.

They were forgetting, she told them frostily. Gemmy was white.

She despised these attempts to undermine her. What especially enraged her was the suggestion that she might not have her children's safety at heart. She would not let them see how they had unsettled her. Calm. Is that what they thought?

They were in a place where there were no sureties of any kind. Of course she wasn't calm! And of course there were times when she was not just scared but petrified, though for the most part she was not, and these weaker moments she kept to herself.

You took slow, shallow mouthfuls of air till the fear drew off.

You took it for granted that life would stay normal, and if you believed that hard enough, it did. Three meals on the table, plates drying on the rack, a wash on the line, shirts, children's things, empty for now but ready to be drawn over your head and stepped into, and hooked and buttoned and soiled and sweat-stained in the time to come.

But there were nights, lying stiffly in the dark, hands clenched at her side, heart thumping, when she did not feel sure.

She was aware of the three children breathing in the dark, two of them her own, the third a sacred trust; the notes of their breathing as different, as distinct one from the other, as their voices, or their bright, quick bodies. What would become of them? What sort of life could they have up here?

She had wanted to give Lachlan a better chance than he might have got at home, but he was wayward, he could go any way at all in this country that was all fits and changes, one thing one minute, another the next. There was no way of telling. Was Gemmy really an influence on him?

It was now, in this loose state at the edge of sleep, or, worse still, of despairing sleeplessness, that her neighbours' doubts took possession of her.

Her mind strayed to where he was sleeping, curled up under a red blanket in his lean-to against the side of the hut; just inches away, the other side of the wall.

Occasionally, in the deep hours, a cry would come from him. Jock would start awake, his hand already feeling for the shotgun; one of the children, stirring, might speak as if in answer, then a second.

She would lay her hand to her husband's arm. He would settle, the child would settle. She would lie there, reaching for breath; wondering what dream out of the dark world he had lived in had come back to claim him or he had gone to meet; which in the open, unguarded state you fell into when consciousness lapsed might have the power to cross from one head to another, to her husband's familiar one on the pillow beside her, where he slept on his back with his mouth open and his fists lightly clenched above his collarbone, or into the fair head of one or other of the children where a pallet shifted with a rustling of shucks.

The stretch of smothering darkness that followed was longer than any stretch of daylight, and space too lost all dimensions. Getting up in the pitch blackness, she would set her foot to the ground, and, with one hand held in front, set off unsteadily for where the water butt stood, ten paces off beside the door. It was like crossing a continent, step by step, with the darkness infinitely expanding ahead and no visible marker on either side. At last her knuckles knocked against wood, she found the dipper, her lips touched a familiar coolness that was like light in her skull.

After such nights, the way back to normality was through habit: matchflare, the worrying of flame out of chips, six mugs unhooked and set down on the table, children, with the puffiness of sleep still on them, not yet come in from the dreams they had been off in, coaxed back to their daylight selves. Little Meg smelling of milk and eager still to cling on, Janet chewing the end of her plait, Lachlan with something distant, almost combative in his look, as if the smoky hut with its familiar objects and smells was not what he had been expecting or was willing for the moment to accept; Jock, as always, finding it hard to get started, elbows on the table, head, all blond tufts, in his swollen hands, the bared neck showing its wrinkles, coarse and pitiable. He would have to shuffle along the form to make room for the girls. He did it without speaking. The girls accepted it. They were used to his glooms. 'Lachlan,' she would say for the second time, but low, not to draw her husband's attention.

The boy, slowly pulling on his pants, would make a face and pretend not to hear. If he held back long enough, he thought, Gemmy would offer to go and split the wood she needed. He would get off.

'Naw Gemmy,' she insisted. Gemmy with his doited look would be stumbling about in a light-headed way, eager at an instant for any task she might have for him, all headlong incompetence, and with no hint of the dark places to which the night might have taken him. 'That's Lachlan's job. Lachlan! If I hae to speak to ye again – '

Jock would raise his head, and Gemmy, hearing the iron in her voice, and fearing the blows that might come – not to him – would hop about in an agony of distress. 'For the Lord's sake, Gemmy,' she would tell him, 'be still noo and drink yer tea.'

She was establishing the precarious order that in just a moment now would make the day lurch and move forward on its ordinary course. 'Come on, lad,' she urged, her tone a little easier, 'stir yersel' and fetch ma wuid.'

80

8

It was George Abbot's custom in the late afternoon to go out with a book, usually a French one, since he was keen, even here where he had no opportunity of practising it, to keep up his proficiency in the tongue. The slim volume in his pocket, its scrolled lettering upheld by putti, represented escape from his own nature and the humiliations and mean insufficiencies of his schoolmaster's existence, but even more importantly, kept open in him, by employing the talents that would be adequate to it, the hope of a kinder future.

He had several favourite retreats. There, the book on his knee and his boots in the dust, he would sit – always alert for ants – in the peppery scent and dull blaze of a tropic afternoon; but his head would be in another place altogether (call it Paris) where the words his soul danced to, *sensibilité*, *coeur*, *paradis*, relieved him of his bear-like heaviness and rough colonial boots, and all around, the scrub, as the word *paysage* lit it, assumed new but familiar colours, then opened in avenues, at the end of which, among drooping foliage, a columned temple glowed, where the crude needs he was assailed by fell away as he stepped into the company of a heroine, demanding but also subtly compliant, with the most delicate wrists, and a delectable, angelic little knowing upper lip, whose name was Ursule, or Victorine.

One day he was tramping along to a place where the entry into this world was easy, when he was hailed by a voice on the track behind him, and when he turned a woman was there, an old woman in brown, rather squat, bareheaded, and wearing boots that were a size too big for her. He recognised her immediately though they had never been introduced.

'That's lucky,' she called. She carried a sack over her shoulder and was dragging behind her a good twelve feet of fallen branch. He stood with his book in his hand and waited for her to catch up.

'Here,' she said, as she came up beside him, 'take this,' and passed the end of the branch to him. 'I can manage the rest.'

He had heard of this. Her name was Hutchence. She lived three miles out on the Bowen road, not in a hut but in a real house, and regularly had a load she wanted carrying or a job out there she wanted doing. The boys and young men of the settlement, Hec Gosper, Jake Murcutt, the older Corcorans, went in dread of being collared and dragged off to dig a ditch or lift a piece of unwieldy furniture. George had believed he would be exempt; that she would see at once, even if she did not recognise him, that he was not a farm boy like the Corcorans or Hec Gosper, to be hailed and commanded. But when it happened he couldn't see how he could protest without appearing foolish; he found himself, as mildly as any other youth of the place, pocketing his book, swallowing whatever mild affront he felt to his dignity, and dragging along beside her.

The branch was heavy, he wondered how she had come so far with it, but he was strong, it gave him no trouble. Only he sweated in his heavy jacket and had, more than once, to stop and mop his brow.

'It's alright,' she told him. 'You take your time. George — is that what they call you?'

She was a tough old body, not quite what she appeared. Though she had too much of the domestic about her to be

82

a source of mystery, he could see quite well that she might present a puzzle. No one knew where she came from – that is, she had vouchsafed no information – or how she could afford to build a real house, or why of all places she had chosen to do it here, or what relation she bore, if any, to the young woman who lived with her, whose name, he knew, was Leona. They had come down, it was said, from the Islands, from Macao, or maybe it was Malacca, and while their house was building had roomed with a widow in Bowen – though no one knew anything of them in Bowen either, save that they had come on the steamer with a whole household of furniture, real furniture of a kind people had never seen, carved chests, wickerwork lounges, three or four elaborate birdcages, and seemed quiet and respectable enough, except for the accent, which the older lady had and the younger did not.

When the house was finished whole troops of people had come out from Bowen to see it; some because it was such a wonder – Bowen, for all that it was a town, had nothing like it; others in the hope that the house, once it was set up, with all the cane chairs in place and the carved chests there to be opened and shown, and the beds made, and one or two pictures hung, might solve the mystery at last by giving away what the ladies themselves would not. But they were disappointing even in this. The house might have flown through the air and landed, plump down, from some seaport up north that they had barely heard of, it was so unlike anything you would see here. If it had information to give away, they couldn't fathom it. It was in a language they could not read.

It was very light and airy, very open. The cane furniture gave it an easy look, but worried them. A chair ought to be solid. All this lacy lightness suggested – but there they were baulked. Their minds stopped short. They sat in the chairs, and from that vantage looked around at the tongue-and-groove walls, which were mostly bare, but no answer came to them. Was it the past or the future they were looking at? If the past, it was not their past. If the future – well, on the whole they did not care for it. Nor did they care for the fact that Mrs Hutchence, once she was in her own home, turned slovenly, as she had not been when she lived at Mrs Blaine's. Her bombazine was all spattered with mud, she wore boots – well so did they, most of them, but *they* didn't live in a house with five rooms plus verandah, with furniture of woven cane, and serve tea in china cups, *bone* china, Bavarian it seemed, or have a daughter or goddaughter, or niece perhaps, or companion, who wore her hair with a comb in it and looked like a large, dark-eyed doll.

Some echo of this had already reached George; so had the opinions of one or two local youths who, for reasons they could not have explained, had at sight of the house felt indignant, as they hadn't been when the old girl first got hold of them. That had been a kind of joke; they had had the advantage of their youth, and of her accent and plain oddity. But the house, floating six feet above ground on its stumps, the cool superiority with which it lay claim to light and air, not to speak of the landscape it stood in, evoked a sense of raw inadequacy in them.

There was an ironwork scraper at the door. They watched and then looked away as Mrs Hutchence dragged her boots across it.

Inside, polished floors that met the soles of their feet with a disturbing stickiness. Most of all, the young woman, the niece or daughter, Leona, whose manner and dress, they had to admit, were wonderful, though none of them could venture what age she might be: 'Thirty at least,' they scoffed when they told of the visit afterwards. She had insisted they sit up at the table, their youth now a cheap handicap, though they were defiant in it, to talk while they drank tea.

Most of them went just the once and turned the occasion,

84

so far as they could manage, into a joke in which it was the house and its two female inhabitants that had been on the wrong side of things. They did not mention the humiliation of the scraper or the strange mixture of embarrassment and wonder that had come to them when they looked back and saw the prints they had left, big-toed and dusty on the boards. If Mrs Hutchence hailed them now – she never forgot a name or face – they went suddenly deaf.

'Well, here we are.'

And there it was, not at all as grand as rumour had it, rather raw and unfinished with its unpainted, corrugated iron roof, but a real house nonetheless, sitting in a patch that had been cleared and scuffled and in the fierce heat was already sprouting weeds.

The columns that supported the verandah roof had bevelled edges, and someone had taken the trouble to give them squared-off capitals. Walls of crisscrossed lattice were set in the arches between, and on either side of the wide wooden steps stood urns, empty as yet, but classic and garlanded.

He dragged the branch, as Mrs Hutchence directed, into the half-darkness under the house, then, surprised to hear a scurry of footsteps overhead, followed her up the steps to the verandah, then on into the cool interior, which he saw, with a start of emotion, was a real room, the first he had been in for more than a year. It was like stepping back into a dream place, though the wicker chairs and little bamboo stands made it too exotic to be familiar. The nostalgia it evoked in him was for a place he might have read about and only imperfectly imagined. So it was a shock when she led him through into the kitchen and he found that of the party they were interrupting, which immediately fell silent, all its members, save one, he already knew.

Gemmy Fairley was there with the two little McIvor girls,

also Hec Gosper, who coloured and immediately assumed, George thought, a hostile air; and standing at the entrance to the corrugated iron recess where the stove was set, Miss Gonzales, as Mrs Hutchence called her before she gave the young woman her other name, which it seemed he was invited to use. 'This is George,' she told them.

'Abbot,' he felt obliged to add.

Hec Gosper dropped his chin to hide a smile. The two little girls, who looked very uncomfortable, pushed their noses into their tea mugs. Gemmy, with a helpless gesture and sounds of inarticulate explanation, pushed past him and fled.

'George has been a great help,' Mrs Hutchence announced. 'Sit down, George. I found a nice piece of firewood, Leona, and George very kindly offered – a cup, Janet. You can choose, pet. Any one you like.'

He seated himself at the pine table, and Hec Gosper shifted to make way for him but remained unfriendly. The older of the McIvor children brought a good teacup and saucer, though the others, he saw, had mugs. Hec Gosper saw it too.

'Well,' he said sulkily, 'I better be off.'

It was Leona who restrained him.

'Dear me, why? Mr Abbot won't mind our bit of fun, will you Mr Abbot? We're all very easy here. We've been telling fortunes – '

Hec Gosper blushed furiously. The truth was that he had, till now, been the centre of such gallantries as the afternoon demanded and had acquitted himself pretty well, he thought. He was mortified that he should now be shown up before this *schoolteacher*. The fortune-telling was all nonsense, an excuse for Leona and him to play little games with one another that the McIvor girls, he thought, were too young to observe.

He was wrong in this. That was because *he* was too young. Janet knew only too well what was going on, and was fascinated, because Hector, she knew, was not much more than seventeen, whereas Leona, as far as she could work out, was – well, twenty-five at least. She knew this because when she was helping Mrs Hutchence down at the hives, Mrs Hutchence talked, and was full of stories about this place and that – they had moved about a good deal – which, if Janet had been able to put them together, would have afforded her larger glimpses of the two women's lives than anyone else had been party to, only she did not have the experience quite to form a picture of travelling gentlemen, some of them ship's captains, or billiard tables, or cooks who had no idea of what Brown Soup should be. She was more occupied, just for now, with the *things* Mrs Hutchence had to show: her china, which was bone china, which meant that when you held a cup up to the light by its delicate handle you could see through it; or the bolts of coloured silk the camphor wood chests were crammed with. These chests were themselves marvellous. They were carved all over with figures so raised that you could close your eyes, trace them with a finger, and still see processions through gardens of cherry trees and willows, with birds among the leaves, and little far-off pavilions.

'Well,' Hec Gosper said, reluctantly accepting to remain and see the thing through. Taking the tin mug in his fist, as if to make clear that he knew, only too well, how he had been slighted, he hid his discomfiture, and his lip, which he suddenly felt the mark of.

Leona saw the trouble he was in. She took the mug he had set down, gave him a look that might have been concili-atory but might also, he thought, be a provocation, and poured him tea from the big blue china pot she hauled from the stove, and as she did so, leaned down and whispered in his ear. Only then did she fill the teacup for George.

'Silly!' That was what she had told Hector in her half-whisper, though they all heard it, and you could actually see the glow that came to the boy's soul. Janet did. She was fond of Hector, and not very fond, after all, of the schoolteacher.

There was a little rise of tension in the room. Leona, standing very tall beside the table, long-necked and with her hair darkly braided, was as overdressed for the occasion, George thought, as he was. They made a pair.

Her frock was of light cotton. 'Freshly laundered' was how he thought of it. Its blue lifted his heart. But his chief impression was that she was scented, and he associated that with the little half-opened rosebuds, pink on white, with which her wide collar was embroidered. The smoothness of the fine-drawn stitches moved him. They spoke of refinements he had thought he might never see again, and as he stared at them, and at the slight lifting of her breasts, he felt once again how isolated he had been in the last months, what a savage he had become. He was happy now to let some of the daintiness of those miniature emblems of 'garden', 'summer', 'home', which he had so much missed, attach itself to the girl; the Englishness too, though her complexion was too dark for it.

Leona wavered. A crease came to her brow. He was something new, this schoolmaster. Even if he was at first sight more awkward than some others, Hector for example, he had a background, he knew something of the world. It embarrassed her that she had been caught out in a game with children, for Hector too was that, however he might stroke his moustache and swagger.

George sensed the little catch of interest in her and felt his confidence lift. If he was let down by anything it was the state of his shirt-cuffs, which were very grubby. He pulled the sleeves of his jacket down to hide them, and noticed, as he did, the dirt that was ingrained in the knuckles of his big hands – even Hector's, he saw, were cleaner. How careless he had allowed himself to become! His hair, for example. He ran his hand through it. It was a bird's nest; whereas

Hector's – Hector was altogether, for all his overgrown limbs and the harelip, very neat, and was not barefooted but wore flash new boots.

George was surprised how keen his return to society had made him. He felt the resurgence of his old vigour, and his soul leapt forward to a time when he and Leona, Miss Gonzales (he preferred to think of her, for the moment, in this more formal way, it set them further apart from the others) would be frank with one another, and tenderly, touchingly close. A conversation in this mode began in his head, and under the influence of the pleasure it provided, his whole being soared, as if the book in his pocket, which he had forgotten, had been transformed along with the rest of him, and was fluttering over the table in the form of a putto with rainbow-coloured wings enclosing a face of quite cherubic innocence, and no discommodious body at all.

Leona, meanwhile, had taken charge of the occasion; in a rather schoolmistressly way, George thought with some amusement. Was she mocking him? If so, he did not resent it. Quite the contrary. He was surprised what a pleasure it was to give in to her authority and be relieved of his own; to be playfully bossed; even if it set him at the same level as Hector Gosper. He had, suddenly, a tender fellow feeling for the harelipped youth that dissolved all rivalry between them in a common response to the rather bantering tone in which Miss Leona softly bound and ruled them. It was a reflection, this, of their shared youthfulness. Hector too bucked up and lost a little of his edgy watchfulness.

The two little girls were astonished by the turn things had taken. They were used to these afternoons when Hector or one of the other boys turned up – it was usually Hector – and the teasing way Leona treated them, but had not expected her to treat Mr Abbot so. Even less that he should accept it, though Janet saw after a little that this was another version of the fortune-telling, only this time the game was between Leona and Mr Abbot.

She saw something else as well. That in playing his part Mr Abbot had no more to do than Hector had. They only thought they were playing, because Leona managed things so cleverly, putting words into their mouth that they had never in fact spoken, and taking both parts herself. Janet was surprised how clear this was to her. The world recently, she thought, kept reaching out to show her things, to catch her attention and enlighten her.

'That's better children,' Mrs Hutchence said, 'that's what I like to see.' She herself had said nothing. She sat listening, but everything, you felt, was contained by her listening, and without it would have been different.

After a time, Mrs Hutchence and Janet went off to attend to the bees. George, Leona and Hector were left alone – but not quite alone. The smaller of the McIvor girls stayed behind, not quite discouraged, George thought, by Leona. She watched them thoughtfully from the end of the table, and when they went out to the back verandah to see Mrs Hutchence and Janet moving about in sunbonnets and veils in a grove below the house, she sat on a woodblock with her elbows on her knees and her chin supported on her fists, missing nothing that passed between them. George wondered if it was just childish curiosity or a kind of jealous love that made her so narrowly watchful, but whether it was for Leona or Hector he could not tell.

Their talk was desultory now. Leona might have been bored with them. There were silences in which George felt at a loss, as if it was up to him now to justify the place she had offered him with some demonstration of gallantry or wit, but the conversation he had begun in his head, which was so full of frankness and intimacy, belonged to the future; he could not catch its tone in the present and he embarrassed himself by asking, out of terror at the gap that had opened, which was too full of the afternoon light and the little McIvor girl's eyes, a question, a direct one, which was in itself of no importance but was put in a manner too blunt, almost brutal – he saw that as soon as the words were out. Miss Leona looked grieved, as if she might, after all, have been mistaken in him. What dismayed him was that he should have *made* such an error, when he was otherwise in a state of such heightened sensitivity.

It did not escape him, even in the midst of his confusion, that a little self-satisfied smile had come to the corner of Hector's mouth, which he was trying to hide by looking very fixedly at his own immaculate boots, while, with his hands in his pockets, he shifted his weight back and forth so that the silence was filled with their cheeping. Was he really, George wondered, the more self-possessed of the two, or was it only that he had discovered, over time, how to fall in with the girl's rather perplexing demands?

But Leona was generous. She did not make him suffer for his lapse. 'Ma,' she began, '– I call her Ma, you know, though we aren't related – Ma,' she went on, 'has taken a great liking, George – she doesn't always, you know. Normally – but why should that surprise you? She's sharp, Ma, very, you'd be astonished at what she can see in people, and at first glance too. She has seen something in *you* – in Hector too, though not in just anybody, she isn't *general*. She sees *into* people, it's a gift. And usually they know it immediately – Hector did, didn't you Hector? – and feel easy with her. That's why we're all so free here. It isn't me, *I'm* not easy. But *she* is, you've no idea. And good too. Wonderfully. She's been wonderfully good to *me*.'

George had no idea what all this meant, and doubted, from the look of him, that Hector did either; but he did feel easy, and understood that Leona was not speaking only for her Ma.

From where they stood at the verandah's rails, he watched that shadowy figure, with the smaller one at her side, move about among the square bee-boxes, loosing clouds of smoke out of her sleeves, and felt a pleasant drowsiness and lack of concern for himself, an assurance that he could leave now and come back, and when he did there would be a place for him.

'I should be off,' he said. It did not bother him that he was leaving the field to Hector, who had, after all, waited him out.

'Well,' she said. 'But you will come again.'

He agreed, and set off over the lumpy yard. He did not have to look back to know that Hector and the tall young woman were watching him go, with the little McIvor girl at Leona's skirts. He was filled with a sense of his own lightness. Some heavier self had been laid asleep in him, and another woken that was all open to the westering glow in which the drab bush trees along his way found a kind of beauty, all their leaves glancing and the earth under them alight along its ridges, and the sky above a show, a carnival, of cloud shapes transforming themselves from forms he could name to others, equally pleasing, that he had no name for, but did not for that reason feel estranged from; he might, he thought, have a name for those later. He had the feeling that there were many things in the world that were still to come to him.

The conversation he had begun back there, he again caught up with. He had been unaware, in his preoccupation with the trees and the sky, that it had been going on all this time at the bottom of his thought. He let it lead him, and was already lost in its pleasant intricacies when he saw, hunkered down beside the track, a figure that startled him at first, and then, when he saw who it was, moved him in a way he had not expected.

It was Gemmy Fairley waiting for the McIvor girls, to see them home. He would have greeted the fellow, and found he was disappointed when Gemmy kept his head lowered, and would not look up to receive the gesture he meant to make.

9

GEMMY FAIRLEY HAD been in the settlement for almost a year. He was working alone one afternoon, slapping fresh planks onto the side of a shed, when he felt the hair on the back of his neck stiffen. He swung round with the hammer raised and they were already on him, two blacks, an old man and a youth, standing quietly just feet away. He had not heard them coming. Making a sign that a white observer would have missed, he dropped his gaze, lowered himself painfully into a cross-legged position, and waited. The two blacks followed and they sat, all three, in a clump, just where they were.

The sign was not visible to Barney Mason's rouseabout, Andy, who was sinking fence posts a hundred yards off on the crest of the ridge; but he did see the rest of it. He had had his eye on those blacks for a good ten minutes.

Watching them emerge out of the ti-tree swamp, the old bloke leading, very tall and thin and gliding like on his feet, he had made a good guess at where they were headed, and laying aside the crowbar, reached for his gun. He followed them all the way down the gully, then, allowing odd minutes for the thick overhang down there, picked them up again just where he expected, on the slope, where Gemmy Fairley's hammer blows were breaking the clear late afternoon stillness.

'Got yez,' he whispered.

If they had strayed even an inch on to Barney's side of the boundary he would have taken a pot at them; he would have felt justified in that. But they did not.

At one point, out in the open, they paused and looked up, bold as brass, to where he stood, pretty well hidden he had thought, and saw him, he was sure of it; any road, recorded he was there. Then boldly turning their backs on him and with no further interest in whether or not he was observing, the old one, high-shouldered and floaty, still in front, walked on. The bloody effrontery of it! The cheek! The gall!

A moment later the hammer paused, he saw Gemmy swing round; and the next thing they were sitting, all three, with their heads together having a powwow. Right there in the open where *anyone* could see them. Didn' even bother to move to the shady side of the shed, as a white feller would, where they couldn' be seen. Just sat like that in the open, maybe twenty minutes, maybe more.

'Oh I kep' me eye on 'em, you can bet on that!' (Andy, in the excitement of having something to tell, was already telling the thing to himself.) 'I seen every fucken move they made, you bet I did. Every fucken move. Then them two blacks got up and went right back on the path they come by.'

For a moment Gemmy had continued to sit; he saw that too. Then, slowly, he pushed himself up, reached for a handful of nails, and it was only when the first hammer blows came flying out across the gully that Andy, with a jerk, came back from the walk his mind had taken, all the way to where it had been hovering about down there, trying to catch what the confab was about, and discovered he had, back here, a fit of the pins and needles, and had to hop about, cursing, till he had worked the feeling back into his leg.

When this last bit of him had returned, he set off, shotgun in hand, at a steady pace – no need to rush – to where the feller was at work again, the sound of the hammer bouncing hard off the hillside and whipping round his ears.

Andy was in a state of high indignation. What he had just seen, he told himself fiercely, was just what he, for one, had all along suspected. The bastard was in touch with them. Always had been, secretly, and was ready now to do it openly. In broad daylight! Just wait, he told himself, till Barney hears.

He had worked for Barney for nearly two years. They weren't close, but he knew Barney; he knew what his thoughts were on the subject of Gemmy bloody Fairley. They were the same as his own. Out of loyalty to his mate, Jock, he hummed and harred and wouldn't admit it, but it showed. He was an open book, Barney. If he got into one of his worrying fits you couldn't miss it. Well, it was a good thing, to stick to your mate – he believed that as much as the next feller. But what about me, he asked himself fiercely, what am *I* then? All I do is bloody work me guts out for 'im, stick up for 'im, keep me eyes open, always thinkin' of their welfare. So why can't you come to me, Barney, like a white man, and come out with what's on your mind. It wouldn' go further.

In the growing hurt to his pride, which was only part of the greater resentment he felt at the many injustices that had been practised on him, he strode fiercely downhill.

Back in Brisbane, in the time after his wife skipped off, he had had a good deal of strife, some of it with the law. He had broken into the chandler's he worked at and stole a few bob from the till – well, six pounds in fact, and done a year in the clink. He blamed *her*. And the Californian – a very smart feller, big talker, who for a time, he admitted, had had an influence over him.

His wife had hated the bloke at first. Jealous! And had

ended up bloody running off with him – what about that, then? Could you credit it? And after being drunk for a week, and getting himself into all sorts of brawls, he had gone one night to the back door of McDowells and broken in and taken the six quid, but why he had done it and how he expected to get away with it, he couldn't say; any more than he could say why his wife, Lorrie, after sounding off for months about what a loudmouth Earl Whitney was, and a cheat and liar, should suddenly up and run off with him. He had known from the start he was the first man they would come after. So how foolish can a man be?

The world was a puzzle to Andy McKillop. He was a puzzle to himself. Two years back, he had come up here just on the off-chance looking for work, and by using some of the fast talk he had picked up from the Californian, who continued to exert a hold over him, had persuaded Barney Mason, who was a decent cove, but soft, to give him a go. He was grateful for that. He had promised himself then that he would never let Barney down, and save for the odd break-out, which left him soreheaded and sorry for himself (he continued to blaze inwardly with a ferocity that only drink, at times, could dull), he had not. He had tried to be a mate to Barney, got sentimentally fond of Polly and the kids. That they were not as fond of him as he would have liked them to be was a disappointment, but he was used to disappointments.

As for this Gemmy – well he knew blacks, he'd had experience of 'em. In his worst period, down there, he had shared a bottle or two with the locals – it wasn't a thing he was proud of, but never mind – and had been off, once or twice, to their camp – he didn't boast of that, either. But it was experience. He knew 'em!

'G'day,' he said with a sour mouth when he reached the shed. He leaned his shoulder against the wall in a very casual manner, but the blast of heat off it got to him through his

96

shirt and he had to shift. It unsettled him, that small mis-
chance, but he recovered and felt descend upon him the large
dignity of one who was here as a representative. 'I see you
been receivin' visitors,' he said, rather pleased with the
understated humour he commanded.

Gemmy was squatting, a nail between his teeth. He looked
up.

Yair, Andy thought, eyes, observing the yellow whites.
Like one a' them. Muddy. Mistrustful.

Gemmy lowered his gaze, and in a leisurely fashion, as if
he was here with only the crickets for company, drew a nail
and slapped it in. The blows flew straight at Andy's skull.
The nail head glinted in the wall.

'Ol' friends eh?'

Gemmy sighted along the plank, which Andy could have
told him was not straight, and took another nail from his
box.

His way with people he did not want to deal with was to
pretend they were not there. He looked right through this
fellow now, this Andy, and he was gone. He disappeared
into the glare off the wall.

Andy huffed. He knew that trick. He had felt the effect
of it before. With his eyes narrowed against the sun and the
shotgun across his arm, he stood his ground, all stringy
indignation. Gemmy squinted at the plank, slapped the nail
in.

That's all right, feller, you take your time. I ain't in a rush.

But personal affront was added now to his anger on behalf
of the others, and with it came a burst of illumination. He
saw what the feller was up to. He was letting on that those
blacks had never existed. That he had never seen them. That
they had never even been here, any more than he himself
was. That they were hot wavering apparitions, produced by
the heat or – at the sickening possibility of his old weakness
coming up again to dog and defeat him, he lost the assurance

he'd had of being a representative here of those who might see him at last as one of them. The sun blazed on his neck. His head throbbed. If I don't get out of the way of this bloke, he thought, he'll bloody nail *me* to the wall. I've got to find Barney. I've got to get in before *he* does – bloody coon!

With a hiss he turned and strode off, afire now with a need to justify himself that was at furnace heat by the time he found Barney. He could barely get the words out.

'Andy,' Barney told him, 'take it easy, eh? Just slow down. What visitors?'

'Blacks. What'd you think it'd be? Fucken blacks!' The words bubbled in his mouth and he swung his head towards the gully, eyes blazing. He punched a fist into his palm. It was such a relief to get them out of his head at last. 'Fucken myalls!'

Barney's lips parted. The dent appeared in his brow.

Good, Andy thought, good. They're in *his* head now.

'They brung 'im something,' he shouted. 'On'y when I went an' faced 'im with it, the crafty bugger'd hidden it, got it outa the way.'

He blinked. This detail had come of its own accord. He hadn't realised till now that he had seen such a thing. His mind must have seen it though, when it took its own walk across there and hovered round them while they sat, because he saw it as clear as day. The whole occasion presented itself to him as the clearest picture, and as it did he felt a widening calm.

'You know, Barney,' he said softly, 'I never did trust that feller. I know *you* never did.'

The word trust was important to him. When it came to his lips he felt the welling of tears. Things would be on a new footing from now on. Trust me Barney. You can. You know you can. That was what his fierce silence expressed.

But if Barney heard the appeal he did not respond to it.

'Oh,' he said, 'I dunno. Gemmy's harmless enough.' The same old song. That was Jock McIvor talk. Andy was incensed.

'Jesus, Barney,' he said, 'didn' you hear what I said? They come to him. Bold as brass. Why? Why did they come? What did they bring him? *He* may be harmless, but *they* aren't, they aren't fucken *harmless*.'

The news alarmed Barney, but he was even more alarmed by Andy, whose sense of outrage, it seemed to him, grew fiercer each time he went over it.

The fact was, things had settled in these last weeks. He did not know what Jock had said to Gemmy, he would not ask, and Jock had spared him the embarrassment of informing him, but he had said *something*. Gemmy no longer strayed where he was not wanted – not by daylight, anyway, though once or twice when he was out last thing at night –

It did not mean the problem had gone away, of course. Gemmy, just by being there, opened a gate on to things, things Barney couldn't specify, even to himself, and did not want to ask about, that worried the soulcase out of him. But for Jock's sake he kept mum. The very last man in the world he would open himself to was Andy. He turned away now, meaning to put an end to the occasion, but as luck would have it Jim Sweetman hove into sight, climbing the long slope towards them. Andy lurched to meet him.

'That feller's been receivin' visitors,' he shouted, all breathless again. 'I was there, I seen it! Hell, they come right up to 'im, bold as brass. Myalls! Fucken myalls!' – the same words, almost, as before, but to Barney they had a different colour now that they were being addressed to Jim Sweetman.

'Some people don't think nothin' of it,' he shouted, 'but what'd they come for, eh? What are they after? If it's two of 'em this time, next week it'll be twenty – '

Jim Sweetman frowned, his mouth tight with distaste at the crudeness of the fellow's speech. He was always half off his head, this Andy. He ignored him and turned to Barney: 'What's he talking about?'

'Blacks,' Andy yelled with genuine outrage. 'Blacks. Fucken myalls, that's what.'

He was determined not to be ignored. He had a savage need to convince people of things; but had first, he knew, and he withered at the old injustice of it, to convince them about himself. He knew that look on Jim Sweetman's face. He had been living with it, in one form or another, all his life. But this time things were different, he had the goods. He got control of the spit in his mouth and started in on his story, and this time, when he evoked the two blacks, he could describe them in every detail; he was astonished himself by what came to him. As if each time he approached the incident it got clearer. When they sat down with Gemmy now, he felt a burning in his right shoulder as if, all invisible, he was leaning right there against the wall of the shed, just feet away, and could see every move they made, hear every word, even if it was some blackfeller lingo they were conversing in. He was inspired.

Barney was astonished. 'You didn't tell me that,' he protested. 'You didn't say that the first time.' It embarrassed him that Jim Sweetman now was taking in every word.

'You never give me the chance,' Andy hooted. 'I tried to, an' you never bloody give me the chance!' His voice was thick with emotion. He was on the edge of tears.

Jim Sweetman looked across at the line of greyish scrub, the last strip of country that was in any way comfortable to him, out of which, if this unreliable fellow was to be believed, with his wild eye and unsteady jaw and the spittle shooting out of his mouth, two blacks had walked in, just like that, as if they owned the place, then walked out again.

His own property was one of the most isolated in the settlement. The edges of it were part of the blacks' traditional hunting ground, and at odd seasons, in the shadowy way of those whose minds you cannot touch, they still passed through it, quietly for the most part. He had no quarrel with them – so far as he knew and so far as any black, once your back was turned, could be trusted; there were a good many white fellers round here, this Andy for instance, that he trusted less. Even now he preferred not to look at the man. He got too much heady satisfaction from being the bearer of ill news. Still . . .

'What do you make of it?' he asked Barney in a level voice. He was thinking of his little granddaughter, around whom his whole world revolved. He saw her wandering off from the safe ground where her mother was hanging out the wash, after a butterfly maybe that kept moving ahead into longer and longer grass. But before Barney could reply, Andy broke in again. 'I saw them give him something,' he said.

That did it. 'Give 'im what?' Jim Sweetman demanded.

'A stone,' Andy said softly, and was amazed himself at the size and smoothness of the thing as it landed slap in Gemmy's hand. 'It was wrapped up like. In bark and that – you know. But I seen it alright. Big as me fist.' And he thrust his closed fist towards them.

A stone. Now how had that come to him? Why had he said that? He sweated. He inwardly beat his open hand against his thigh and cursed. That stone, when they went to look for it, would prove difficult to locate; and Jim Sweetman, for one, would want to see it.

He had been afraid that Gemmy would accuse him of seeing things, and what had he done? He'd given him the chance to prove it. It was always the same. He always went that bit too far. When the stone was looked for and failed to appear they would start to wonder, their voices take on a sceptical tone and the sort of sly derision that leaves a man no way out but to insist, and dig deeper into his own grave. 'Been seein' things again have you, old son? Sufferin' from a touch of imaginitis, are we?' There was no pity in people.

Well, if it came to the test he would stick to his story and let them choose. Between him and this blackfeller. When push came to shove, they'd choose *him*, they'd have to. Only he wasn't sure of it. His bowels went soft in him.

And the stone, once launched, had a life of its own. It flew in all directions, developed a capacity to multiply, accelerate, leave wounds; and the wounds were real even if the stone was not, and would not heal. Andy McKillop felt miserably that he was the first victim of it.

He mooched round the settlement with his head down, scared silly by what he had achieved, and sat at times looking at his closed fist and telling himself that when he opened it, by some magic he did not believe in, it would be there, solid, graspable. See? See? You'll believe me now, I reckon. He would make them recognise it at last, as proof of the non-existence of that other, heavier and more fatal thing, an imagination.

But best of all, he thought, might be to tip his head back and swallow the bastard as if he had never coughed it up in the first place.

10

WITHIN AN HOUR of the blacks' visit Jock had news of it. First from Ellen, who looked serious – she had heard it, in a panic, from Polly Mason – then, as he expected, from Barney, who could barely hold in the exasperation he felt.

Jock felt sorry for him. He was being pressed from all sides: by Polly, by Jim Sweetman, and as always by his own unhappy sense that the world was preparing at any moment to tear away from him the last vestige of security. Jock, however, was determined to insist for as long as he could that there was a reasonable centre to things, though he too had been shaken in these last months; not by what Gemmy threatened but by what he had begun to see in others.

Barney looked miserable. Usually when he came to Jock it was for consolation, and he was looking for it even now. He was alarmed by what he had heard, since Polly was; but what mostly upset him was that he had been shown up in front of Jim Sweetman. He came striding. But there was something in Jock's steady calm that made the words he had been preparing all the way uphill go dry in his throat. When he spoke it was mildly.

'Yes,' Jock admitted, 'so Ah've heard.'

'Well?' Barney said. There was a whine in his voice that was very nearly childish. He wanted to be let off the hook. 'It's what we been worried about all along. You know that. No use pretending you don't.'

'Ah'm nae pretending,' Jock said.

'I mean – they just walked right in, in full daylight. Bold as brass – ' Jock gave him a hard look, as if he knew that the words were the same ones Andy had used, and Barney was embarrassed to hear in his voice something as well of Andy's thin, self-justifying tone. 'I mean,' he said, in a voice closer to his own, 'they didn't seem to mind *who* saw 'em. Neither did Gemmy. Andy says – '

'Andy?'

Barney felt the colour rise to his throat. 'Look here, Jock,' he said, 'don' play me about, eh? I'm not the only one, you know.'

Jock turned away. Andy he could ignore, but he resented this appeal on Barney's part to the mob who stood behind him. A sense of loneliness came over him. He did not want what was happening here.

But Barney, who felt he had put himself on the wrong foot, was defiant. 'Jock,' he said, 'I won't be fobbed off. Not this time.'

The sense of distance between them was new, and it seemed to Jock to hold the possibility of a terrible desolation. None of the old assurances would cross it. To attempt them, he saw, would be to insult Barney by making too little of what it had cost him to risk a break between them. They meant a good deal to one another.

'A'richt then Barney,' he said, as coolly as he could manage, 'Ah'll speak to him. Tell Polly no' to worry. Trust me.'

He might have left it there, on that note of appeal to what was intimate between them; but some imp of irritation in him, some wish to register, at least, the hurt he felt, made him speak again. 'They went off, dinna they?'

'They did, yes. They did. But there's this – this thing they brought 'im? This *stone*.'

'Wha' stone?'

'They brought him a stone. Didn't you know that? Andy says – '

Andy again! Jock blazed up. 'For God's sake, Barney, dinnae gie me what Andy says. Andy's a mug, ye know that. Dinnae throw Andy at me!' He controlled himself. 'So what's a' this aboot a stone? What's it supposed to be? Magic? Is that what Polly's a' workt up aboot? For Guid's sake, man, ye've got a shotgun!'

They met one another's rage in a little shocked engagement, then glanced away.

Jock's defiant scorn was false and he knew it. The shotgun he had evoked to balance that other threat had no weight. The two forces were not equal; not in his own head nor in Barney's either, certainly not in Polly's. He had brought them to the very edge of it; of a world where what was cleared and fenced and in Jock's own terms reasonable – all their education, their know-how, yes, and the shotguns they carried – might not be enough against – against what? Some vulnerability to the world that could only be measured, was measured still, by the dread it evoked in them?

'Barney,' Jock said, and he felt a coldness at the bottom of his brain, as at some gathering darkness in himself and all around him, 'this is madness, ye know that. Andy's a ratbag. For God's sake, man, when did ye ever tak heed o' what Andy says? We're no' scared o' stones. Ah thought that was the difference between us and them. What's it supposed to do, aeneway, this *stone*? Soor the coos' milk? Set haystacks on fire?'

He was trying to make light of the thing, but the very spit in his mouth went dry, and when the words were out, in a voice he barely recognised, he regretted them, however light they might be, as if, in the urgency of his attempt to beat Barney down, he might have set forces in action, out there, just by breathing into the air the mere possibility, that he could not deal with any more than Barney or any other man.

'Look Barney,' he said, sickened that they had come so far, 'Let me talk to him, eh? Gie me that much. And dinnae let me hear denny more' – he could scarcely bear to make another reference – 'aboot myalls, and magic and – '

But he did hear – from Ned Corcoran – and lost his temper, and was sorry for it, since he saw in the other men's faces a kind of hardness – did his defence of Gemmy go this far? – at what they saw as a disturbing confirmation of change.

Was he changed? He saw now that he must be, since they were as they had always been and he could not agree with them.

When had it begun?

When they agreed to take Gemmy in. That was the simple answer, since it was from that moment that some area of difference, of suspicion, had opened between them. But the more he thought of it, the clearer it seemed that the difference must always have existed, since he too was as he had always been; only he had been blind to it, or had put it out of his mind from an old wish to be accepted – and why not? – or a fear of standing alone.

He had never been a thinker, and he did not now become one, but he began to have strange thoughts.

Some of them were bitter. They had to do with what he saw, now that he looked, was in the hearts of men – quite ordinary fellows like himself; he wondered that he had not seen it before. What the other and stranger thoughts had to do with he did not know.

It was as if he had seen the world till now, not through his own eyes, out of some singular self, but through the eyes of a fellow who was always in company, even when he was alone; a sociable self, wrapped always in a communal warmth that protected it from dark matters and all the blinding light of things, but also from the knowledge that there was a place out there where the self might stand alone.

Wading through waist-high grass, he was surprised to see all the tips beaded with green, as if some new growth had come into the world that till now he had never seen or heard of.

When he looked closer it was hundreds of wee bright insects, each the size of his little fingernail, metallic, iridescent, and the discovery of them, the new light they brought to the scene, was a lightness in him – that was what surprised him – like a form of knowledge he had broken through to. It was unnameable, which disturbed him, but was also exhilarating; for a moment he was entirely happy.

But he wondered at himself. A grown man of forty with work to do, standing dreamily stilled, extending his hand, palm downwards, over the backs of insects, all suspended in their tiny lives in a jewel-like glittering.

Another time, by the creek, he looked up, casually he thought, and saw a bird. It was balanced on a rounded stone dipping its beak into the lightly running water, its grey squat body as undistinguished and dusty looking as a sparrow's (but there were no sparrows here), its head grey, with a few untidy feathers.

He was sitting, himself, on a larger stone, also rounded, eating the last of a sandwich, his boots in mud.

But what his stilled blood saw was the bird's beak drawing long silver threads out of the heart of the water, which was all a tangle of threads, bunched or running; and his boots had no weight, neither did his hand with the half-bitten lump of bread in it, nor his heart, and he was filled with the most intense and easy pleasure: in the way the air stirred the leaves overhead and each leaf had attached itself to a twig, and whirled yet kept hold; and in the layered feathers that made up the grey of the bird's head; and at how long the threads of water must be to run so easily from where they had come from to wherever it was, imaginably out of sight, that they were going – tangling, untangling, running free. And this time too the intense pleasure he felt had a disturbing side.

The things he had begun to be aware of, however fresh and innocent, lay outside what was common, or so he thought; certainly, since he could have found no form in which to communicate them, outside words.

His wife missed very little of this. She knew it went against his nature to be at odds with his friends and to be thrown so much on his own thoughts. It worried her to see him brood, and once he had begun, to see how bitter it made him, as if, once opened, that gate led to darker places than he had meant to venture into or had known existed.

She too was distressed that they had drifted so far apart from their neighbours; neighbours meant a great deal up here. She had recognised before he did the change in people's attitude. She defied it – that was her nature – and in doing so, perhaps, made it worse. She had even perhaps, in her indignation, encouraged in him a view of his friends that he might not have discovered so easily, or so soon, if he had not seen how hurt she was. She was sorry for it now. She had not meant to make things hard for him.

But the sense of being wronged drew them together. She could not be sorry for that. They found consolation in one another, and things to say, not always directly, that restored an intimacy between them that she had missed in the harshness of their life up here.

He had turned his full gaze upon her – that is what she felt. He wanted to know now what her life was beyond what he saw and had taken for granted, a shirt washed and shaken to make it soft, food on the table; to enquire into her affections. It was amazing to him – that is what his tentativeness suggested – that he had known so little and had not looked. There were times now when the intensity of his looking made her blush.

It was as if they were at the beginning of a courtship, very delicate, almost fearful on his part, and it struck her that in the early days of their knowing one another he had not been like this – he had been too sure then of winning her, or she had let him see too quickly that he had done so. It had prevented them from discovering something essential in one another. She was wiser now. She let him go on, and felt like a girl younger than she had been in those early days; more hopeful too.

'D'ye think aften o' hame?' he asked one evening.

They had walked, as they often did these days, to the top of the ridge, where they could stand at the boundaries of their own land, which had grown clearer to them in their recent difficulties. It was just on sunset. All the western sky was drenched in flame, and the daylight moon, the wrong way round, hung colourless, almost transparent, in a blaze of such resplendence that you felt small, almost dwarfed before it. He turned his face to her and was transparent himself.

She knew what his question intended. In these last weeks he had begun to wonder if their coming here, that great irreversible act that had determined so much in them and in the lives of their children, had been a mistake. Home, suddenly, seemed very close to him.

He had turned his gaze from her and was looking, very intently, at a little flower he must have plucked as they walked, which grew on a bush that was very common here – they were standing in an unruly tide of it; a kind of pea-flower, very satiny white and small, which it would be easy to miss. It was the way he held it, the grace of the bit of a thing in his rough hand, and the attention he gave it, that

109

touched her and made its whiteness come alive. When she looked round the whole slope was shining with it.

What could she tell him?

The conditions of their life up here were harder than any she could have imagined at home because they were so different. Even the openness she had longed for was a frightening thing. There had been a comfort in crowdedness and old age grime and clutter that she only appreciated when it was gone. If it was easy here to lose yourself in the immensities of the land, under a sky that opened too far in the direction of infinity, you could also do it (every woman knew this) in a space no longer than five paces from wall to wall; to find yourself barging about the hut like a trapped bird, clutching at whatever came to hand, a warm teapot, a startled child, a shirt with the smell of sweat on it, to steady yourself against the cyclone that had blown up in the gap between you and the nearest bedpost, and threatened to sweep you right out the door into a world where nothing, not a flat iron, not the names of your children on your lips, could hold you down against the vast upward expanse of your breath.

She had known such occasions, often, often. The children saw them in her and kept clear. It was the fearful loneliness of the place that most affected her – the absence of ghosts.

Till they arrived no other lives had been lived here. It made the air that much thinner, harder to breathe. She had not understood, till she came to a place where it was lacking, the extent to which her sense of the world had to do with the presence of those who had been there before, leaving signs of their passing and spaces still warm with breath – a threshhold worn with the coming and going of feet, hedges between fields that went back a thousand years, and the names even further; most of all, the names on headstones, which were *their* names, under which lay the bones that had made their bones and given them breath.

They would be the first dead here. It made death that much lonelier, and life lonelier too.

What she was homesick for, not always, but on some days, in some weathers, were the two little graves she had had to leave down there on the Downs, in the newly dug black soil under the big, foreign trees, with no one to visit them. That had been the real break; deeper than leaving Airdrie, or crossing the sea in the knowledge that she could never go back.

Time and again, in her loneliness, even with her other children about her, she went and stood there among the rusty fallen spikes and monkey-puzzle light, gazing down at the rain-streaked stones with the names and dates, hoping to look up and find that he too had come. But it had never happened. If he came there on occasions, and she thought he did, their times had never coincided. All this was something they did not speak about, because there was too much space, up here, between words, even the simplest, as there was between objects.

But that was another of the changes. She felt sometimes, as now, that they stood together there beside the two little humped places in the ground.

'Ah miss Kate,' she said very quietly. 'And Alex.'

He nodded. He was turning the little white pea-flower in his hand. Then he bent down and placed it, very tenderly, on one of the mounds.

'Oh, and a thing Ah saw once, a tightrope walker – ' she felt no oddness in the transition. 'He had a rope fae wan side o' the street t' the ither, and he walked on it, in baggy troosers, wi' a bar in his han – ' She held her hand out, balancing, and took a step or two above the earth. 'It wid be grand to see something,' she said.

What she meant was to have something so rare, so

111

miraculous even, to show the girls, as her father had shown her. (It was her father's hand she had held when she looked up breathless to see the tightrope walker, with his slippered feet, walk.)

'Where was it?' he asked.

'Airdrie.'

'How auld were ye?'

'Seven. Eight maybe. Aulder than Meg.'

'How did he do't? Show me again.'

She showed him. Held her arms out and took three steps, very slowly, raising one foot then the other, over the rough earth with its sticks and dried leaves, as if she were walking thirty feet up in the air.

He followed her with his eyes. Then reached his hand out and caught hers, as if he was afraid she might fall.

'Ah'd gie aenethin' t' hae seen it,' he said. 'You, Ah mean. T' hae seen you.'

11

GEMMY'S VISITORS HAD appeared on a Thursday. In the days that followed one or two little things began to go wrong around the place. None of them was unusual, but that they should happen just now, and that there should be a string of them, was unsettling. Accidents, Jock told himself. Coincidence. He was trying hard to hold on to the normality of things, to resist in himself the wave of panic and suspicion that was running uncontrolled through the settlement. He did not believe the bit of trouble he was having was the work of blacks, and it had not yet occurred to him that it might be a neighbour. He and Lachlan fixed the break in the fence – he did not involve Gemmy – and he kept to himself one or two later breaches in the daily run of things. But when three of Ellen's geese were found with their throats cut, and the stones of their little yard all alive with greenflies and sticky with blood, the enormity of the thing could not be concealed.

The geese had names. One was Hereward the Wake, another Jemima, the third Lucie. The children were broken-hearted, but frightened too. Who could have done such a thing? Little Meg, through her tears, gave him a look that went right through him. He had been powerless to protect Jemima, so why not her, or any one of them?

He was shaken. Who was it? Who could have done the thing? He looked in one man's face, then another's, and could not tell, or what was worse, save himself from the poison now of suspecting each one of them. He was a stunned animal, all his strength, now that he was staggering, the weight that might bring him down. Ashamed to admit to his friends, even to Barney and Jim Sweetman, what was happening, he chose not to go out.

Lachlan was full of outraged defiance. 'We dinnae have t' tak this,' he insisted.

He wanted Jock to demand of him some proof of absolute affection. He would defend them, the household, his uncle's honour, their blood, no matter what. 'Just tell me what,' he told Jock, who was touched by the boy's fierce loyalty, 'and Ah'll do it. Ah'll kill them.'

But when he looked a little and saw what it might mean, he too fell quiet. The idea that they should draw in close behind an invisible stockade and pretend that nothing had been done to them was shameful to him; but even more shameful was the business of admitting before Jeff Murcutt and the Corcoran boys that they had been set apart, and could be so openly terrorised.

Once again the responsibility, Jock felt, was his. It's a'right for me, he thought, but he's too young for this.

His aunt too saw it. 'Lachlan,' she told him gently, though she too was bitter, 'we've done naethin' wrang, you know that. We've done naethin' to be ashamed o'.'

'Ah'll kill them,' he repeated, 'gin Ah find who 'tis.'

As for Gemmy, he simply vanished; not into the bush, as one or two fellows predicted, but into his own skin, behind his own dim but startled eyes. He knew what was happening and that he was the cause of it.

One morning early, three days after the slaughter of the geese, Jock was making his way down the slope towards the gully when he came upon Gemmy half-running up the track towards him, wild-eyed and stumbling as if someone, or something, was after him. Jock put an arm out to stop him, but Gemmy shot him a look, of desperation Jock thought, and ran on. He called after him but he did not turn. Jock went on, and the feeling of dread that came over him was like the faint, far-off smell of some new violation that was on its way towards them. He came to the foot of the track, and there it was.

Just where he should turn off and enter the gully was the shed Gemmy had been mending when his visitors arrived, the new planks in its wall, the new nail heads showing plainly in the weathered grey of the rest. And there, smeared across them, was a stain, a gathering of greenflies that heaped and bubbled, and the air that came to his nostrils rich with its stink. Someone had plastered the place with shit. Someone else – Gemmy he guessed – had tried to clean it off with a handful of grass but had only succeeded in spreading the filth.

He stared and his gorge rose. Snatching up a handful of dry grass, he smashed at the loathsomeness of the flies that were feeding on it, as if the abomination was in them. They leapt away, but some of them, drunk on foulness, were caught and smashed. He threw the soiled grass from him and sank to the ground. Drugged himself, he began to roar through his clenched teeth and his body swayed.

The flies returned. They climbed over one another's backs in their eagerness to feed and wallow. He felt maddened that such creatures should exist in the world, and would have rushed once again to smash them. But what had they to do with it? Some man had done this. That was the real abomination. Someone he knew. Someone whose eyes he had looked into, and recently; maybe at the very moment when he was planning the thing. That fellow had squatted here, somewhere here – he swung about again as if he might catch the glimpse of a retreating shirt-tail – and with a grunt of satisfaction squeezed this filth out of himself, fouled his own hand with it, and spread it as an insult between them, made public and stinking in the sun. He saw the hand with its load of filth moving across the wall and understood now

115

that what it was setting there was a word. What word? He shook his head wildly to prevent it forming, to prevent the possibility of it getting in there, of himself giving it form, and was glad that the only other man who had seen it was Gemmy, who could not read. To have that word in his head, where it could never be scrubbed out, would be madness to him. Even now –

He got to his feet and went swiftly to the creek, his breath racking him like a wounded animal's, and stumbled into the smooth and liquid light (it was the same spot where he had seen his bird), and scrubbed his hands, and would have stripped and scrubbed his whole body, but discovered that he had no belief any longer in the water's power to cleanse.

What horrified him was that he might find himself face to face with the man whose smell he had on his hands, in his head too, a thing so intimate, so personal, that surely he would recognise it on the man himself, and the word would leap up in the air between them, taking form from the stench. He swung about again. And it seemed to him now that it was the sky that had been smeared, the earth, the water. The word was on them; some old darkness out of the depth of things was scribbled there forever, and could never now be eradicated.

12

ANDY MCKILLOP'S visionary powers were greater than he knew. The blacks had brought Gemmy something, though it wasn't a stone.

When all the proper formalities had been exchanged, and the necessary questions asked and answered, the silence between them as they sat, all three, and faced one another, became a conversation of another kind; and the space between them, three feet of baked earth where ants in their other life scurried about carrying bits of bark and other broken stuff in the excited scent of a new and foreign presence, expanded and became the tract of land up there under the flight of air and the stars of the night sky, that was the tribe's home territory, with its pools and creeks and underground sources of water, its rock ridges and scrub, its edible fruits and berries and flocks of birds and other creatures, all alive in their names and the stories that contained their spirit, for a man to walk into and print with the spirit of his feet and the invisible impact of his breath.

For longer, much longer, than the ten minutes Andy McKillop counted from his side of the hill, they moved together through its known places. And Gemmy — as he recognised one and then another feature of it, the site of old happenings, strange encounters, or stories, or lean feasts — felt the energy flow back into him, and saw, in the sudden access of it, how weak he had grown in these last months, with the dry little cough that plagued him, and his stomach troubles.

The air he breathed here did him no good, the food too. The ground he walked on jarred at every step. The land up there was his mother, the only one he had ever known. It belonged to him as he did to it; not by birth but by second birth, by gift, and not just for his lifetime either but for the whole of time, since it was for the whole of time that it existed, as he did too so long as he was one with it. This was what the blacks had brought him, in case he needed it. They were concerned that in coming here, among these ghostly white creatures, he might have slipped back into the thinner world of wraiths and demons that he had escaped, though never completely, in his days with them. They had come to reclaim him; but lightly, bringing what would feed his spirit.

They spread the land out for him, gave him its waters to drink. As he took huge draughts of it, saw it light his flesh. Watched him, laughing, bathe in it, scooping great handfuls over his breast. In the little space of dust between them as they sat, they danced, beat up clouds, threw rainbows over their heads. Then they rose, exchanged the formalities of parting, and went. A day and a night it would take them to reach a place that was already humming all round him as he took up his hammer and sent the blows of it leaping with such clarity in the release of his spirit that they might be flying, he thought, thirty miles off, like stars his arms could fling over the furthest ridge to light their path.

Then that bloke Andy appeared; came stumbling out of the scrub with his crooked jaw and restless, runaway eyes, and stood leaning on air, with the odd, empty look that anything, any madness might fill; hinting, demanding. The air around him was immediately infected, sucked into the emptiness he made just by stepping into it. Gemmy felt the good health that had been given him weaken. As if he had looked into a pool – that was how this Andy affected him

– and seen an image of himself that was all unfocused pieces that would not fit.

With an effort he pulled his eyes away, and the man, or the furious emptiness rather that wore a look and held a shotgun and was trying to find the *shape* of a man, went still and vanished.

It was the kind he was, this Andy. If you refused him your attention he mumbled, dithered, boiled with his own hopeless impotence, and disappeared.

But when, with a hiss, he did turn on his heel at last and stalk away, Gemmy felt his heart fall. He was real enough; the emptiness was real. And they stood too close to one another on the lowest rung of things in the settlement for his ferocity to accept defeat.

Slowly, over the months, he had learned how to handle such fellows. He stepped into their skin, looked about quickly, stepped out again, then dealt with them as they dealt with themselves.

One or two of them knew this and kept clear. They did not care to be exposed, even to themselves. Others felt it but did not know, and the less they knew the more openly hostile they grew; these were the ones you had to watch out for. He watched, allowing himself no illusions, and since there was a kind of agreement among them, or so it seemed, that open savagery was not permitted, he survived.

He had no real tormentors here. Even the crudest among them affected a bantering tone – though he soon saw through it – as if any mischief they might get up to was an expression of an irresistible jollity, and when it went too far, and he was roughly used, the fault, if anyone's, was his. They got him to his feet, brushed him down, told him he wasn't hurt, that he was a good fellow and that they had meant no harm. (It was true. They thought they didn't.)

His real tormentors were in his head, and they came after him more and more often now as their shapes rose clearer in his memory and grew faces and fists in the dark hours of his sleep. And as always, it was Mosey and The Irish who were the worst of them: Mosey with his high thin voice and fair wisp of a beard, soft as a girl, and The Irish with gunpowder pits in his cheeks and two fingers gone from his right hand.

'What have we got here, now? A boy, is it? By Jimminy yes, I reckon it's a boy, a boyo. But what a scrawny, thin-necked, weasel of a boy,' and with each new taunt they would begin to push him back and forth between them, 'what a snub-nosed – '

'Red-eared – '

'Big-mouthed – '

'Low-arsed – '

'Knock-kneed – '

'Imitation of a boy it is! More like a scrap of old cheese – '

'Or the sole off me boot – '

'Or a bit of stale pie crust you can't hardly get your teeth into – '

'Than a boy, a boy, a boyo!'

all the while leering and lunging as they sang the words back and forth and bowled him back and forth between them, till they began to thrust about under his clothes, and the cries that broke from him as their fingers pinched and poked and teased and twisted were the cries of a child, but the pain now was that of a grown man, outraged and powerless, who had to stand by and see it done, and for all the fierce howls that came out of him could neither drive the devils off nor prevent what, in a moment now, unless he wakes, will be past all remedy . . .

He wakes from such a dream. A clammy hand is over his mouth, a mouth, close in the dark but not his own, is roughly panting. He struggles; half waking, jerks his body to get free, but as so often, the dream hangs on, tough arms hurdle his ribs. It hangs on just that breath longer than sleep, but the

120

breath, indrawn, is very deep and the fear comes to him that this time he may not be able to shake it off, that the tormentors he carries within him, who have been so long hidden and have begun, more and more often now, to come to the surface in him, will this time break clear, get out into the real world, where he will have no more control of them than he had in the days when they were real and he was one of them.

And it is true. This time it is true. He is awake, and these others, all knuckled hands and shoulders and rough heads and breath, are cramped close under the lean-to with him, shoving, whispering instructions, at one point giggling.

They have got him hooped about with their arms, they are pulling a bag over his head, and with the choking chaffy roughness of it against his mouth, and in the dry breathlessness of nightmare, he is being hopped and dragged over stones, and when he stumbles, jerked upright by a crowd of bodiless whisperers who are trotting along on all sides of him, as if all his tormentors had found one another at last in the dream-space of his head, and discovering now what they have in common, have joined forces to gallop him to some corner of the dark where he is flat-handed this way and that, and when he throws up his hands to protect himself, falls, but at other times merely hovers on the brink, and is baited and played with; not brutally but with hands, neither fisted nor frenzied, coming at him from every direction, and without sound save for the grunted effort it takes to haul a man to his feet so that he can be knocked down again, and the breathing in the darkness, which is huge even inside the sack, of many mouths.

Suddenly there is water round his ankles, and when he stumbles this time there is a splash that scatters moonlight through his skull.

His arms are jerked back, his head pushed down. His head, roaring into the sack, is thrust under water and the darkness in the sack turns to mud. He gasps mud. Then goes under again, and yet again, till a voice rises in protest. The others say hush, but it changes things. The grip on his arms weakens.

He is released and on his knees in the creek when he hears a voice he does recognise: Jock's. It is shouting.

A scuffle, the barging all round him of bodies in the dark, and the next moment he is upright, gasping, breathless inside the sack, and the sack, muddy and streaming, is torn from his head.

13

E LLEN MCIVOR STIRRED. From the other side of the wall had come one of those nightmare cries that were so much part of their nights up here that she did no more at first than pause in her half-sleep and listen for the disturbance it might make among her children. But on this occasion there was more. A series of bumps against the wall itself jerked her into full wakefulness. She put her hand out, touched her husband's arm in the dark, and he started up, his hand on his shotgun. Rolling out of bed he went to one window, then quickly to the other, as she, her heart swinging wildly, put her foot to the ground. One of the children woke. It was Janet. 'Shh,' she said, rising quickly now.

The child sat up with her eyes wide in the darkness and looked to where her father crouched at the window, his face tense in the faint light from out there, the barrel of the shotgun softly aglow. 'What is it?' she breathed.

'Shh,' the voice came again.

Jock was puzzled. He saw a muffled group, but it was making away from the hut, not towards it, in an awkward, shuffling way that he could not understand; a huddle of four, maybe five figures.

He handed Ellen the shotgun and began to pull on his moleskins and boots while she, with the shotgun ready, took his place at the window. She could see nothing out there. The group was swallowed up now in the darkness further down the slope and she wondered what he had seen that disturbed him.

He took the gun, touched her hand lightly in the half-dark, gave her a warning look to be quiet, and slipped the latch of the door.

'What is it?' Janet asked again.

'Shh, ye'll wake the ithers.'

Going to the door, she opened it a crack, letting a flood of moonlight in, and a medley of night sounds, but nothing more.

'It's naethin',' she said. 'Gae back to sleep.'

She had opened the door just wide enough to slip through, and barefoot now, just as she was in her nightgown, she stepped out, dropping the latch behind her.

Careful not to wake Meg, who slept beside her, or Lachlan, who was already mumbling, Janet set her foot to the ground and crossed quickly to the door. Very carefully she raised the latch, and barefoot like her mother, ventured out into the strangeness of the yard.

It was transformed, made unfamiliar by moonlight and the tinking of night-creatures. Big clouds overhead seemed closer than any she had seen by day, and the ground, which her bare feet knew well enough in sunlight, felt odd, not quite safe. She was aware of every pebble in the unevenness of it.

Her mother was standing very still about halfway down the slope, her nightgown shifting a little and the dark of her body outlined within it. She was struck by the heaviness, the solidity it suggested, and a sudden affection for her mother, which she did not always feel and seldom expressed, came moistly into her throat so that she was tempted to call her. The material of her mother's nightgown was all agitated moonlight, but the body inside it was dark, bulky, deeply rooted out there. Though exposed, it did not seem vulnerable. She had a flash of her own body, dark and thin inside her nightgown, but was exhilarated rather than afraid.

There was no sign of her father, or of whatever it was that had drawn him out, then her mother, then her.

She stood without breathing, or so it seemed, and the calm she felt, which was all suspense of ordinary, daytime feeling, had to do with the tense and brittle strangeness with which the world was touched, which might have more to do, she thought, with some quality she had brought to it out of her sleep than with the play of clouds across moonlight.

I am the one who is seeing all this, she thought.

That, as much as anything, accounted for the nature of what she saw. And with it came another thought: Me, not Lachlan.

She was aware suddenly of being outside in the dark, while the other children slept on in the house.

Not for a moment in all this did she think of danger.

Her mother turned and started up the slope, then stopped a moment, looked back, then came on again; and when she saw her standing in the dark there, outside the door, did not chide her.

They stood side by side and watched her father and Gemmy come up the hill, Gemmy stumbling, her father with one arm round the man, supporting him. Her father raised his head and the look he gave them she would never forget.

He led Gemmy by them and to his sleeping place against the side of the house.

'Janet come awa' noo,' her mother coaxed, touching her lightly, not perhaps for the first time, 'come ben, come to yur bed.'

When Jock McIvor reached the bottom of the slope, it had been to see no more than the last shadowy retreat of whoever it was. They were gone across the creek. He could hear them crashing through the scrub on the other side. There was no point in following. He had Gemmy to deal with, who was drenched and quaking, and had to be half-carried up the slope.

What he had dreaded most when he had come rushing downhill was that he would have now to come face to face with them; they would stand in the open at last. They had saved themselves, and him too, by making off. Cowards, he thought bitterly. But wasn't he one too in the relief he felt? He was shaking, but comforted Gemmy as well as he could and for the first time did not draw away when the man clutched and held on.

Looking up about halfway up the slope, he saw his wife. He did not want to face her. She saw it and turned away, and went to where Janet was standing, barefooted at the door.

That was when the real fear, the real anger took him. That in the middle of the night his wife and daughter should be standing out under big clouds at the edge of the dark, hanging together and watching him drag a helpless creature, half out of his wits, back from a moment of senseless bullying, while the men who had done it – neighbours! – were creeping home to crawl in beside their own wives, safe in bed.

He went on past them and dragged Gemmy into the shelter of the lean-to. Laying aside his rifle, he crawled with him into that musty, dark-smelling place, and did a thing he could not for his life have done a week, perhaps even an hour ago: he sat huddled close to him in the dark, and when he shivered, drew him closer, pulled the old moth-eaten blanket round the two of them, and with the man against him, heard his juddering breath, and smelt it, while outside moonlight fell on the cleared space round the hut where his wife and children waited.

Janet lay awake in the dark and it was a long time before her father came in.

She heard him undress and climb into bed, and for a moment they whispered, but she could not make out what they said. In the morning, grim-faced and slow as he always was, her father had nothing to say and she knew that whatever it was that had happened, which she had seen and not seen, she must not ask about.

Once, during the day, her mother came very quietly and kissed her, as if in recognition of something between them that the others were to be kept from, even Lachlan; but she did not know what it was, and when she looked up expectantly, her mother did not enlighten her.

Perhaps the gesture had been meant as a consolation. But for what?

The place where her mother's dry lips touched her brow glowed, and for a long time afterwards she was aware of it, as if, at that point, a kind of knowledge had been passed to her.

It was the moment she would think of later – more even than the more ordinary and alarming one that came soon after – as the true moment of her growing up.

14

S*MALL FIG OR plum with oval, dark-green leaves, the* *milky juice of its young shoots being efficacious in healing* *wounds. The scraped root-bark of another plant (the* Ourai *or* Grevia) *is used to make a poultice: large alternate, oval* *serrated leaf with a small brown berry, generally in pairs,* *on a small axiliary pendicale.*

Barkabah: *broad-leafed apple tree with pink and white* *flowers, the fruit full of seed and tasting a little like dried* *banana.*

Small, creeping leguminous plant that runs in and out of *the grass,* Kardolo *in the native tongue, with a blue flower* *like that of cultivated tea: three narrow long sharp-pointed* *leaves upon a common stalk, with a root not unlike carrot.*

These entries in Mr Frazer's field notebook give no indication of the conditions under which they were made. Their clear copperplate, the lines as straight and orderly as a row of cabbages in a Berkshire field, and the details of the drawings that accompany them, do not suggest that what is being recorded belongs still to the untamed wilderness or that the man who is at work on them – a large man in a collarless shirt, the wide-awake hat laid aside for the moment but leaving a red line across his brow under the sweaty scalp – has for the past hour been plunging uphill over rough ground and is now settled on a log in a tropical clearing to set down, in all the excitement of new discovery, what he has just been shown.

To achieve the meticulously detailed drawings and the

almost pedantic notes, he has to keep hand and heart steady. It is as if, in disciplining himself to the demands of the work, he has broken through to a cleared place in his own nature where these plants are already installed behind glass.

Gemmy, watching, is solemnly impressed. His tongue, following the movements of Mr Frazer's hand, works at the corner of his lips as if it too had a part in the business. The drawings for him have a mystical significance. They are proof that Mr Frazer, this odd whitefeller, has grasped, beyond colour or weight or smell, the *spirit* of what he has been shown. Watching a plant emerge, the swelling bulb or fruit, the perfected leaf, Gemmy is entranced almost to breathlessness, his own spirit suspended as the real, edible object, in its ghostly form, breaks out of itself onto the whiteness of the page.

The accuracy and attention belong to Mr Frazer's dogged side. Since the day he made his first pot-hook he has known that he is a plodder; that if he is to keep up with the tumbling complexity of things he must pay closer attention than others to every detail. But he adopts quite a different mode when, under the hiss of the evening lamp, he takes out his writing-up book and lets himself loose in the realm of speculation. The lines run crooked then and might come from a different hand, as thought leaps, darts away up sidetracks, doubles back, stops amazed at its own discoveries, dances, kicks its heels up, delightedly tumbles:

We have been wrong to see this continent as hostile and infelicitous, so that only by the fiercest stoicism, a supreme resolution and force of will, and by felling, clearing, sowing with the seeds we have brought with us, and by importing sheep, cattle, rabbits, even the very birds of the air, can it be shaped and made habitable. It is habitable already. I think of our early settlers, starving on these shores in the midst of plenty they did not recognise, in a blessed nature of flesh, fowl, fruit that was all around them and which they could not, with their English eyes, perceive, since the very habit and faculty that makes apprehensible to us what is known and expected dulls our sensitivity to other forms, even the most obvious. We must rub our eyes and look again, clear our minds of what we are looking for to see what is there. Is it not strange, this history of ours, in which explorers, men on the track of the unknown, fall dry-mouthed and exhausted in country where natives, moving just ahead of them, or behind, or a mile to one side, are living, as they have done for centuries, off the land? Is there not a kind of refractory pride in it, an insistence that if the land will not present itself to us in terms that we know, we would rather die than take it as it is? For there is a truth here and it is this: that no continent lies outside God's bounty and his intention to provide for his children. He is a gardener and everything he makes is a garden. This place too will one day, I believe, yield its fruits to us and to the great banquet at which we are guests, the common feast; as the Americas brought corn and tomatoes and sweet peppers, and rhubarb and the potato, that bitter root of the high Andes that women, over long years, by experiment and crossbreeding, have leached of its poison and made palatable, to be the food of millions. (There is a lily-root here that the women know how to boil and make edible.)

The children of this land were made for it, as it was for them, and is to them a rich habitation, teeming with milk and honey – even if much of its richness is still hidden; but then so was the milk and honey of the Promised Land, which was neither milk, in fact, nor honey, and the land itself to all appearance parched and without promise. We must humble ourselves and learn from them. The time will come when we too will be sustained not only by wheat and lamb and bottled cucumbers, but by what the land itself produces, tasting at last the earthy sweetness of it, allowing it to feed our flesh with its minerals and underground secrets so that what

130

spreads in us is an intimate understanding of what it truly is, with all that is unknowable in it made familiar within.

Pausing a moment, he draws back from where his hand, running on ahead, has taken him further than he meant.

He is aware of the lamp's hissing; of his wife, her head, under its cloud of hair, bent over the music she is reading through; and beyond the sill, the night, stirred by the clapping of wings, the inaudible puff of seeds as they spread, the random but orderly couplings and killings of a nature different from the one he was used to at home, yet the same.

Since earliest childhood, botanising has been his one sure refuge. With the loneliness of an only child among nine brothers and sisters, he had discovered that the world of plants offered an order he would never find among men. Even the idea of *family* seemed most moving to him as it applied to specimens as wonderfully different to the eye as the apple and the rose.

He was a night wanderer. Slipping out in the dark he would track night-scented flowers in the summer woods, or, with breathing suspended and his whole body alert, observe from a hide, in the soft night air and a liquid light with its own colours, the life of creatures that were abroad, as he was, while the human world slept. That was the joy of the thing. While the eyes of others were closed, or open only on the fanciful world of dreams, to look in on a part of creation that is secret, but only because it lives in another time zone from that of men.

Night creatures, night-flowering plants. They touched on what was hidden in his own nature; and it occurs to him, as he plunges through the undergrowth with Gemmy, or strides knee-deep up a slope, that in a way he is still at it. This, from the point of view of where he began, is the night side of the globe. He has found it at last, can explore it now in full sunlight. Is that why his discoveries here mean so much to him?

He turns back a moment to his notebook, and what he sees is no longer a wild place but orchards in which, arranging themselves in rows, wild plum and fig and apple have moved into the world of cultivation, and in the early morning light, workers with the sun on their backs hang from ladders and reach out to pluck them.

The theodolite, he writes, *offers only one way of moving into the continent and apprehending the scope and contours of it. Did we not, long ago, did not our distant ancestors, bring in out of the great plains where they wandered, out of mere wilderness, the old coarse grasses that lapped the bellies of their horses, and, separating the grains and nursing them to plumpness, learning how to mill and grind and make daily bread, and how to tend the wild vine till its fruit yielded wine, create settled places where men and women sit at tables among neighbours, in a daily sacrament which is the image of the Lord's greater one? All this can be done again. This is what is intended by our coming here: to make this place too part of the world's garden, but by changing our-selves rather than it and adding thus to the richness and variety of things. Our poor friend Gemmy is a forerunner. He is no longer a white man, or a European, whatever his birth, but a true child of the place as it will one day be, a crude one certainly, unaware of what he has achieved – and that too perhaps is part of His intention: that the exemplum should be of the simplest and most obvious sort, deeply moving to those who are willing to look, and to see, without prejudice, that in allowing himself to be at home here, he has crossed the boundaries of his given nature. Of course, such changes inspire in the timid a . . .*

He breaks off, his hand pausing above the inkwell. He has come to a knotty place in his reflections, feeling a lapse of the high emotion that has carried him on.

One day, not long ago, returning from one of his afternoon excursions, he came upon Jim Sweetman with his granddaughter on his shoulders, a pudgy child of three, rather spoiled and with eyes so deep in her fat little cheeks that you caught only a glint of them as she jerked her legs and crowed. The old fellow was prancing about in circles, lifting his head and dancing left and right as the child directed.

Still in the excited state his excursions aroused in him, he hailed the man, and they stood a moment on the path while the child, sulking, jerked her legs, impatient to have her grandfather go back to being a pony. Jim Sweetman, patiently, set his hands over her knees, and still half-attending to the child's call upon him, and a little put out himself, perhaps, at the interruption to their play, listened, accepted the hard little fruit he was offered, though not the suggestion that he should bite into it. So he himself did, and showed the man the seeds.

Jim Sweetman did not light up with the vision of orchards. He seemed embarrassed in fact, and at just that moment the little girl drove her heels into him.

'Stop that now,' he said, more sharply perhaps than he meant. 'Grandpa's talking.'

The child's face collapsed. She took a breath, and Jim Sweetman, feeling the change of weight in her little body, lifted her down on to his arm.

Too late. She had begun to shriek, and very satisfied with the effect it produced, she continued, and would not be pacified. He had stood by, waiting for the child's passion to exhaust itself. He had forgotten what fierce, self-willed little creatures children could be. It was so long since he had had any of his own.

The child shot a glance at him, shrieked again, and Jim Sweetman, stricken, while the child sobbed into his breast, shook his head at him as if *he* were responsible. If the man recalled anything of the occasion it would be the little girl's grief. The hard little fruit he had been shown meant nothing to him.

133

Jim Sweetman, for all his lack of imagination, was the best of them. He knew better than to try the rest. Being caught, once or twice, coming in with Gemmy, he had seen the look in their eyes, and felt Gemmy, who missed very little in this way, fall away from his side — intending, no doubt, kind creature that he was, to protect him.

If he is to get any response to his schemes he must go higher; that's what he has learned. Farmers grasp only what they already know. So, with no notion as yet who it is intended for, he has begun writing what he thinks of as a 'report'.

He looks again to where his wife, just feet away, sits with a score in her lap, her head bowed over her music. She turns a page, her hand going to catch a wisp of hair that has come astray.

'What is it?' he asks, as if he heard a faint burst of what she is playing in her head. 'Is it Field?' But she does not look up. She has not heard him over the wave of notes.

He is in the habit of turning pages for her while she plays — or rather, he was; she has no instrument up here. It is the first time in all their moves that he has been unable to provide one for her. She does not complain; though music, he knows, is her refuge from the frustration she sometimes feels. With *him*, with his passionate confusions. She saves herself by taking no part in his interests, perhaps out of a fear of finding them foolish, and he in turn keeps out of hers. He does not interfere in the letters she writes to their girls, and to the boy, Edward, except to add his greetings at the bottom of a page. And if he dips at times into the things she likes to read, articles on political economy and the like in the journals she receives, it is not because he hopes to share their arguments with her, but, in a tender way, to catch a glimpse of where she has been, and what it might be there that has excited her. He reads over such passages, and their underlinings, with a deep pleasure, though often enough they have no meaning to him. Only in music, when he turns the pages and sees precisely where her fingers have arrived at in the score, is he quite certain of her emotions and his own, and feels they are one.

They have been married for thirty-three years. She has followed him in his progress – or decline – halfway across the world, and further each year from her real life, which is, he knows, in their children. She is cleverer than he is but does not make him feel it. Cleverness, she knows, has nothing to do with what he is after; which is revelation. What will be revealed, he believes, is the unique gift that is in each man and woman, in each creature and plant too – what else has his study of nature shown him? – and must also be in him: a gift he alone can give to the world, and which without him it must lack.

She sits with the music spread in her lap. The piece has come to an end. Quickly, feeling his gaze, she looks up, makes a face, not at all the face of a woman in her sixties – a child, it might be, playfully poking a tongue at him – then places her hands on her hips, leans far back from the waist, and yawns.

The other women in the settlement found the minister's wife poky. It had got about that she was the cousin of an earl, maybe a duke, and they had hoped for glimpses in her of the romance of birth, even in the reduced form, up here, of a silver milk jug or a set of crested spoons. They wanted a hint in their vicinity of pride, high custom, refinement. That the Frazers were poverty-stricken was no impediment. That was *his* fault.

But she fulfilled none of these easy expectations and might even have set out, in her brusque way, to thwart them. She was a small freckled person, though fine-boned, with a mass of hair that had once been red-gold and was now rusty and none too well controlled. She was dutiful enough in her enquiry about the health of children, but did not always remember their names. Once a month she received a parcel of books and other papers from one of her daughters, the elder one at Aldershot (the other lived at Poole and there was a son in Canada who taught school), which she herself went into Bowen to collect and would immediately, right there at the steamer-wharf, tear a corner from, like a child with a loaf of bread; she was so hungry for its contents.

They would have liked to send their girls to her to be improved with a little needlework of the fancier kind, but she had no skill with a needle, even, as you could see from Mr Frazer's shirts, in the plainer way of buttons and hems. Many of them, poor as they were and with no claim to gentility, were better managers than she was and had a higher regard for what they thought of as the refinements. The one thing you could say of her was that she did not give herself airs. They would have complained if she had, but when she did not they felt cheated of the bit of colour she might have shown them, which would have been a greater comfort here than absent-minded kindness or charity.

'I want to speak to you about something important,' she says from the bed while her husband is still undressing. He looks surprised, then comes in his shirtsleeves to sit beside her. He loves these late moments of intimacy between them.

'Charlie, something very serious has happened,' she says, 'you mustn't be upset.' She goes back a week to Gemmy's visit from the blacks, then, too quickly for him to quite make the connection, to the attack at the McIvors'.

He feels the blood come to his cheek. It is only partly indignation and a kind of shame at so much baseness; there is also the personal embarrassment of having it brought home to him, yet again, how out of touch he is. He has heard nothing of this; seen nothing either.

'Who can have done such a thing?'

136

His wife does not reply. Today the men of the place, shamefaced perhaps, have kept out of sight. It is the women who have been busy.

'I know you believe there is no harm in the man,' she tells him, 'and I'm sure you are right. There is none. But people are afraid. There is harm in that. It would be best – Millie Sweetman thinks so, and she is a very sensible woman – if he were put where they can do him no harm. Where he wasn't quite so – visible. Of course, the best thing of all would be to send him away altogether – to Brisbane, if it could be arranged. But in the meantime – I've already spoken to her – Mrs Hutchence would take him in.'

So it was arranged. No one, not even his wife, has thought it worth consulting him.

'Charlie,' she says gently. She takes his hand. 'It had to be done as quickly as possible. The McIvors can't be left with him, they've already suffered, and there are children to consider. It's true there's no harm in him, but he *is* a danger just the same. Not through his own fault, poor fellow. It was best to let Millie Sweetman take over – people will accept that. And you know what Mrs Hutchence is,' she adds lightly. 'They won't try their nonsense with her.'

But the heaviness on his heart will not shift. His one consolation is that he knows at last what he must do, and who his report is for.

15

WHEN THEY WERE working with the bees they worked in silence. That was how Janet thought of it, though in fact Mrs Hutchence kept up a continuous slow talk – it was the only time she did – which was not meant to tell you things – that was all by-the-way – or to do anything at all in fact but be a soothing noise in which the bees, Mrs Hutchence herself, and she as Mrs Hutchence's helper, were gathered in a single breath into an activity that required this overriding soft babble to contain and settle them.

Mrs Hutchence would have been surprised if you had told her: 'That was a funny story – the one about the Chinese pirate.' She would have denied she had ever told it, and wonder, perhaps, how it had got across from *her* head, since the event or the memory of it might indeed have been hanging about there, into yours. When she was silent she often thought she had said something – it could cause difficulties that, Leona certainly thought so – but when she *had* said something she was, as often as not, unaware of it.

This business with the bees was like no other. Something in you slept while you were at it and you woke refreshed, which was just why Janet loved it and why the bees, now, were a necessity to her, as if without them she could never enter into her own thoughts. She felt too that Mrs Hutchence was her first and would always be her greatest friend.

The old woman had a strange effect on her. Under her influence the world slowed to a pace she could manage at last: by which she meant that she had time to *see* things, to let them enter her and reveal what they were. It was a beautiful effect, this. Without it she did not know how she would ever have discovered certain things or believed they existed.

They had come to Mrs Hutchence through Gemmy, who had been called to make hives for her, and since he knew about these things, had once or twice gone into the bush and found swarms of the little stingless native bees she kept along with her imported ones.

The first time they went to visit her Janet had been carrying a present her mother had sent: a bowl of mutton jelly with a sealing of solid fat, and to keep the flies off, a crochet cover weighted with beads. With Meg trailing behind and the bowl held in both hands before her, she had walked slowly down the long road out of town, found the house, which they both marvelled at, mounted the stairs to the verandah, called into the still, dark interior, and when they got no reply, set off downhill towards the gully and its hives.

They saw Mrs Hutchence from far off, looking unfamiliar in a bonnet and veil, with her skirts hiked up and her big boots flopping. Billowy clouds of smoke issued from her sleeves so that she herself was shadowy, and the bees, where they passed through the slanty sun-shafts, were dazzling sparks.

Janet knew what she was doing, there was no mystery in it. But the scene, just the same, touched on something, just at the edge of thought, that she could not catch hold of. She would have liked to set the bowl down, relieve the ache in her arms, and concentrate on the spectacle and the slight disturbance it had set up in her, which was not at all unpleasant; but she could not risk it. Ants were already scurrying around her feet, engaged for the moment in hauling off dead bees, but alert already, the explorers among them, to what she carried. She had to use first one foot, then the other, to brush them off.

So she stood holding the bowl just yards from where Mrs Hutchence was working, with Meg, who was not sure about the bees, sheltering behind her; and in fact one or two of the most adventurous of them did come and settle on the crochet cover, and roll about there, and light at last on her hands. Mrs Hutchence, she thought, was singing; though it might have been the bees, which were exploding in separate points of light, then rushing together in clumps. The smoke reached their nostrils. Meg sneezed.

'Goodness,' Mrs Hutchence exclaimed, 'who are you, child?' seeing only one of them. She came forward. Bees were tumbling in the folds of her sleeves and dotted all the front of her veil. 'Don't be frightened.'

'I'm not,' Janet said. Her stiffness had to do with the way her arms ached from holding the bowl.

'An't you now.'

Mrs Hutchence gave her a hard look.

'Well you needn't be, either. The smoke makes 'em sleepy, you know,' and she sent a little puff towards them.

'Dear me, there are two of you.'

They came often after that, and were introduced to the house and its treasures, but for Janet the real attraction was Mrs Hutchence and the hives, which looked so closed and quiet under the trees but were filled with such fierce activity – another life, quite independent of their human one, but organised, purposeful, and involving so many complex rituals. She loved the way, while you were dealing with them, you had to submit yourself to *their* side of things.

Meg, on the other hand, was attracted to Leona. Janet too enjoyed the company of the kitchen table, with its games and teases, but it was the hives that drew her more. If she could escape, she thought, just for a moment, out of her personal mind into their communally single one, she would know at last what it was like to be an angel.

This thought belonged, yet did not, to what she thought of as her 'visions' but was more reliable than those, more down to earth. They had a worked-up quality to them; she worked them up out of *herself*. This came from outside and had begun when she saw Mrs Hutchence at work for the first time.

She associated her feelings at that moment with the ache in her arms, and with the bowl and its two covers, the one of fat, the other of crochet weighted with beads, which had kept her earthbound if she had been inclined to float; but mostly with the sound the bees made, the single vibrant word resounding in their furry heads, the way it gathered and magnified, so that she understood immediately not just *what* they were, in their individual bee bodies, but *why* they were; the flow of the honey and its making out of pollens gathered from all the surrounding country – the stringybark blossoms, the banksias, the eggs-and-bacon bushes they grazed on, the swamp-water they drank – to become the heavy scoop of gold in the bowl of a spoon, and the transparent thread from which, in its slow falling, it hung and did not fall.

She became Mrs Hutchence's helper, with a sunbonnet and veil of her own, and soon was as expert, almost, as the older woman. But by then, the event had occurred that was to settle her in this business; and for life.

It was on a day not long after Gemmy had moved into the little room there, so she was no longer a beginner. They had finished their work with the bees. She had put off her bonnet and veil.

The day had been unusually oppressive, steamy, and for

141

the last hour a dull sky had been glowering, bronze with a greenish edge to it, that bruised the sight. Suddenly there was the sound of a wind getting up in the grove, though she did not feel the touch of it, and before she could complete the breath she had taken, or expel it in a cry, the swarm was on her, thickening so fast about her that it was as if night had fallen, just like that, in a single cloud. She just had time to see her hands covered with plushy, alive fur gloves before her whole body crusted over and she was blazingly gathered into the single sound they made, the single mind.

Her own mind closed in her. She lost all sense of where her feet might be, or her dreamy wrists, or whether she was still standing, as she had been a moment before, in the shadowy grove, or had been lifted from the face of the earth.

The bees have their stomachs full, her mind told her, they will not sting. Stand still, stand still. It was her old mind that told her this.

She stood still as still and did not breathe. She surrendered herself.

You are our bride, her new and separate mind told her as it drummed and swayed above the earth. Ah, so that is it! They have smelled the sticky blood-flow. They think it is honey. It is.

Mrs Hutchence was only feet away. So was Gemmy. She could hear their voices calling to her through the din her body was making. But it made no difference, now, the distance, three feet or a thousand years, no difference at all; or whether she was a girl (a woman), or a tree. She stood sleeping. Upright. A bride. Then the bitterness of smoke came to her throat, and the cloud began to lift; and there, through the gaps in herself, was Mrs Hutchence with coils of smoke pouring out of her sleeves, and Gemmy, open-mouthed with a frame in his arms, and the bees, one by one, then in fistfuls, rolling off her, peeling away like a crust, till she stood in her own skin again, which was fresh where the air touched it, and only a few dozen foolish creatures were left that had got themselves caught and were butting with their furry heads and kicking, in a panic at being alone.

She felt Mrs Hutchence's hands on her skin now, which was quite clear and unharmed but seemed new to her, and all through Mrs Hutchence's fearful ministrations and Gemmy's whimpering cries, she remained a little out of herself – half-sleeping, regretful, her two feet planted square on the earth.

Years later she would become expert beyond anything Mrs Hutchence might have dreamed of at the bee business. She would know all the breeds and crossbreeds, and create one or two new ones – actually bring them into being, whole swarms that the earth had never known till she called them. She would devote her life to these creatures, bringing to the daily practical study of their habits and all the facts and lore that is the long history of their interaction with men, a bodily excitement that went back to this moment, under the trees, when her mind had for a moment been their unbodied one and she had been drawn into the process and mystery of things.

For it was not the bees themselves that had claimed her; they had been only the little winged agents of it, the little furry-headed, armed angels that might, if she had panicked, have stung her to death, martyred her on the spot, a solid, silly giant that had stumbled in among them.

All that was still to come. For the moment, still numbed by the shock of what had struck her, she moved to comfort Mrs Hutchence, who had sunk to the ground, and sat like a rock gone suddenly soft, and sobbed and took a good while to get her breath.

'Don't be upset Mrs Hutchence,' she said, feeling the older by years, though her voice was unchanged. 'The bees didn't hurt me, I knew they wouldn't. I remembered what you told me and it was true. They didn't sting.'

She saw then, from the look on Mrs Hutchence's face,

that though her own faith had been absolute, Mrs Hutchence's had not.

So it had been *that* that had saved her, the power of her own belief, which could change mere circumstance and make miracles.

She went, half-dreaming, and looked at the hive, all sealed now, a squared-off cloud, still drumming, that had once been clamped to her skin, a living darkness, so that the only light came from inside her, from the open space she had become inside the skin they made of living particles, little flames.

She had remained cool inside, and when the flames drew off what was restored to her had a new shape, was simpler; she had emerged with a new body, which the world – and this was the point – had dealt with to its limit and let go, and which, from now on, however things might appear, it could not destroy.

She was rather surprised really that she did not *appear* changed to Mrs Hutchence, since the body she was now standing in, as her mind saw it, was not at all the old one.

She looked past Mrs Hutchence to where she had stood just a moment back, and what she saw was not herself, not a gawky child in pigtails and a faded frock, but a charred stump, all crusted black and bubbling; and she saw it – this, when she met his astonished look, was what convinced her – through Gemmy's eyes.

16

G EMMY, SUFFERING FROM bruised ribs and a broken mouth, but even more from a bruising of the spirit that threw him into moments of frantic terror, was given a room at Mrs Hutchence's, a little back room so small you might have stood in it and touched your fingertips to either wall, but clean, freshly painted and cheerful, the women thought. It did not occur to them that its very spareness, its being so light and open, yet enclosed, might prove frightful to him. Once the door was shut he did not know where to set himself between its close walls.

There was a cot where in his first days in the house Leona sat beside him and fed him soup and tried to make sense of the stumbling stories he had to tell; also a chair with an embroidered cushion, and a low little chest of drawers. From the beginning the chest was a worry to him.

He believed at first that the discomfort it caused him, the sense that assailed him of his spirit being touched and interfered with, must come from something Mrs Hutchence kept there. Leona was astonished one day to find him sitting in the midst of a snowstorm. He had taken the sheets and pillowcases they kept in the drawers, hauled them out, dragged them round the room, and then tried, very ineffectually, to stuff them back again. What could have possessed him? Was it a tantrum? Something *they* had done? Mrs Hutchence reproved him, but lightly – she did not want the poor fellow upset – and they spent a whole morning with their sleeves rolled up and the copper boiling. To make sure there was no repetition of the trouble, Mrs Hutchence found a place for the things in her own room. The little two-drawered chest stayed empty. But Gemmy by then had discovered what it was that had touched him.

It was the smell of the wood, which was quite unlike that of any of the local timbers he had to do with, and the moment he understood it, he stepped out of the room, out of his present self, into a clearing that had always been there, he thought, just waiting for him to stumble to the centre of it. And there he stood again with fine wood-dust raining down on his head, mixing with snot to clog nostrils and throat.

Back, far back, before Willett, when he was still at the maggot stage, he had been one of an army of little shitty creatures, mere bundles of rag and breath but with hands that could clasp a broom and strength enough to push it, whose job it was, for all the hours of daylight, to crawl about in the low place under the machines in a timber mill, sweeping sawdust into wooden pans. Fine wood-dust poured incessantly from the teeth of the saws – that was the smell – and there was another, heavier smell, which was that of the oily grime round the base of the machines and the bolt-heads that fixed them to the floor, which they picked out with their nails, mixed with sawdust, and ate. He had never since tasted anything so good. Overwhelmed, he stared at the object, the little pinewood chest that came no higher than his thigh, the same height he had been then, which had brought all this back to him.

When darkness fell in the close little room, it stirred; the smell moved towards him and the screaming of the machines returned that all day had deafened them so that even when they were stilled the screaming in their heads went on. He would feel about in the darkness then for the others. What part of the world had *they* got themselves to? Their sharp little elbows and knees had poked through his flesh. When

146

they curled up in close heaps together between the legs of the machines, among snufflings and breathings and bubbly murmurings, their communal heat and breath was a thing his body had never forgotten or known again. Where were they, his fellow maggots? What had they turned into when, at five or six, he had discovered the shape of an ancient, undernourished child and become Willett's Boy? All night his body sought them in his sleep.

So the room began to work its magic on him. Sweating between walls he entered a different sleep from the one he had known in the lean-to at the McIvors and in his years with the blacks, a sleep that belonged to a different life and produced different demons; the kind that live in rooms.

It is a fearful thing to be faced in the dark by a pair of cracked leather boots, all their eyeholes torn, their laces trailing, the loose tongues charred and smelling of flame.

The boots are Willett's. They are empty. Touched with flame, they sit propped up in front of a grate. Willett has just stepped out of them, and in his stockinged feet, one big toe showing, is padding round the room, filling it with his richness and the rumblings of his voice. Willett. Source of unquestionable commands; of curses, blows, growls, slobbery kisses. The first being he has memory of. Before Willett there is only darkness, his life as a maggot, the giant legs of machines. In a moment he will turn his attention from Willett's boots, which it is his job to place in such a way that they dry but do not scorch, and there, in the reflected light of the fire, Willett himself will stand, red-haired, gigantic, with his shaggy brows and a voice that can creep about in every corner of a room, the fiery god–demon and ruler of his world, whose touch and smell and breath is on every object he puts his hand to.

The boots? Willett's. The long clay pipe that he is allowed, when Willett is in the mood, to take a slow drag on? Willett's.

The blackened pan is for cooking Willett's supper, a nice fat sausage, and provides his own supper too, in the grease he scrapes from it with his finger or with a crust of bread.

Willett's razor strop. Which he has experience of on Saturday nights, when he uses it to whet Willett's razor – more intimately, if he has been playing up, when Willett gives him a lick of it across his back. Then there is the cake of soap that gives Willett's hands their smell, a choking sweetness.

He is Willett's Boy, as the boots are Willett's boots. He has nothing of his own. Everything that comes to him comes through Willett, including his name, Gemmy, which is what Willett calls him when he is not just 'Boy'.

Willett is a rat-catcher, and they have a bulldog, Ketch, and two ferrets. If the ferrets have names he has forgotten them.

Having known no better life than this, he cannot imagine one. Willett provides the only bit of closeness he has ever been offered, and since he has nothing else to love, he loves him with a fierce intensity, a fear too, which is the greatest he knows, that he may get lost, or that Willett one day may abandon him, taking with him the whole world as he conceives it: Ketch, the ferrets, the streets Willett is king of, the razor, the sweet garden smell of his hands, his curses, his kisses, the warm grease of the skillet, the boots with their trailing laces and tongues lit with flame, his name, Gemmy, his claim to existence as a boy, as Willett's Boy.

In one corner of their room is a heap of keys of every shape and size, some as long as his forearm. Willett adds to them each week by poking about in the boxes outside rag-and-bone shops, or in the market barrows along the canal, weighing this one or that in his palm, turning it in the air and chuckling. He has never been introduced to the rooms, or chests or little boxes the keys unlock. They are part of a life, he believes, that Willett keeps secret from him. He can only think that while he is asleep at night Willett must slip off to one or other of those rooms and sit gloating over the contents of the chests or boxes that lie open before him, but what they might contain he cannot imagine: things that exist in parts of the world he has not seen, that Willett has not revealed to him.

He pinches himself to stay awake. He will follow Willett and see where he goes. But he is too tired. The moment his head touches the sacks he sleeps on he is asleep. He imagines that he has stolen one of the keys, found the room it opens, then a box, and with the lid of the box closed over him, lies with his hands folded in the dark, not daring to breathe, waiting for Willett to appear. He hears the door of the room open. Hears Willett's boots dragging. Sees a crack of light as the lid is lifted, smells the sweet garden smell, squeezes his eyes shut in the dark, waits for the voice: 'Ah, boy, so that's where you've got to.' Waits and waits. In one of the drawers of the chest, in the clean little box of a room at Mrs Hutchence's with his hands folded on his breast, his cheeks wet with tears, barely breathing.

Six days a week, rain or shine, they go to the park, Regent's Park. Willett's job is to clear its ponds of rats. His job is to go in with the ferrets, then, at the end of the day, to see that the animals are caged and watered, to dry Willett's boots, polish the brass on Ketch's lead, and, when all is done, to slip out in the early light of the gas-lamps and fetch ale for their supper.

Among so many barefoot urchins slipping in and out of the crowd – up to no good, on the lookout for mischief – he has a place, he is Someone's Boy. The jug he carries is the guarantee of that; empty on one leg of the journey, so that he can skip along as he pleases, full and in danger of slopping on the way back.

Very happy, since he is of a cheerful disposition, to be free for a little among the noise and many interests of the streets, he ducks and dodges among the crowd, leaping out of the

149

way of carriage wheels on the slushy cobbles and cursing the drivers; when it freezes keeping an eye on the rumps of the standing horses, or the donkeys in coster's carts, for the wink of an arsehole and the load of steaming shit that comes tumbling; then diving in quick to get the good of it, the lovely quick-fading warmth between his toes. He may stop a moment, not long – Willett can be a devil – to see the blood from an accident, or two punks, urged on by a mob, beating the daylights out of each other, or a tinker at work with a little *tink-tink* hammer and a bit of fire in a tin, or to trade insults with his friend the hot-muffin man, or catch snatches of music outside a penny-gaff.

As a sideline to the rat-catching trade, Willett supplies rats for weekend matches. As Willett's Boy he gets pennies for drawing the rats out of their cage, which is a basket with an iron top, and tossing them by handfuls into the ring.

He is used to rats, but it is a mucky business. Willett, very dandified in a red handkerchief and brushed hat, rubs him beforehand with caraway oil, and pets and cajoles, and urges him not to look feared, and if he draws back (out of sight of the gentlemen, of course) whispers hoarse threats, which he knows he can rely on, and pinches him hard under the ribs. But he *is* afraid.

When he plunges his arm into the musky dark and hauls the sewer- and ditch-rats out of the hot, drain-smelling interior, they squeal and tumble over one another's backs, and fight, using their teeth something horrible, and he gets many wounds that turn to open sores. He has scars all over his hands – one thumb is bitten through – and on his ears as well, since the rats, if they get the chance, will run up his body like squirrels up a tree trunk and fix their claws in his hair, till Willett untangles and tears them off. They get up the legs of his trousers too if they are not laced at the knees with string.

He is a game little fellow – that is his reputation. He is

proud of it, and has learned to swagger and win cheers. Only at night, when he curls up on his pile of sacks, the rats appear in great numbers and huge size in his dreams, and if he yells and wakes Willett he is thrashed. So he sleeps with one of the ferrets under his shirt, in the belief that the smell of it will keep the dream rats off.

That is his life. He can imagine no other. He fusses, in his anxious, old-mannish way, over Willett's needs, takes pride in their housekeeping and their catch, and pleasure in what bits and pieces of entertainment he comes by in the streets. Willett is an easy fellow when he isn't drunk or in one of his dumps. They have rare times together. Especially when Mag is with them, who is Willett's moll, and sometimes, on Willett's suggestion, when they've all been drinking together, takes him on her lap like an overgrown baby, and gives him her breast to suck, and, to Willett's vast amusement, frigs him under his shirt till he is squealing. But one night, after a beating no worse than others he has received, he waits till Willett is snoring, and, still heavy-headed from the beer they have drunk, gets up, lets the ferrets out of their cages, sweeps a heap of rubbish into the middle of the room, finds tinder, and lights it. There, he thinks as he watches it catch. He could not say what he has in mind. Nothing, perhaps. He is eleven or twelve years old and some darker nature has begun to emerge in him. He has resentments.

He stands watching the smoke make wavery threads. They twine and thicken. When the first little jigging flames appear, a smile comes to his lips. Now a lively redness is playing on the walls, the flames jump in play, so cheerful and full of change that he is held in a state between dreamy contemplation and an excitement that makes the hairs rise all over his body. He breaks off and goes, in an easy unthinking way, to where Willett lies and kicks him. Perhaps he intends to show Willett how changed everything is, to share with him what he has achieved. Willett growls. He does not stir.

151

The ferrets are running now, tumbling over the backs of chairs, leaping at the walls, the redness bristling on their backs. He too begins to be alarmed. The flames are taller than he is. He runs at them and stamps a little but burns the soles of his feet. Snatching up a rug, he tries to stifle them, but they shoot out from under it, and the rug too catches, showering sparks. He has to throw it in with the rest. The whole room is aglow. It sweats. Grease runs down the walls. The ferrets are mad things under his feet. At last, with smoke thickening all round him and choking in his throat, he can think of nothing else to do but throw the window open, and, as the cold air rushes over his shoulders and the room gives a roar behind him, leap out into the night, and run, and keep running till he passes the last street he recognises and where anyone might recognise him.

It does not occur to him that he has stepped off the world. The streets he is moving through are cobbled, have corners to turn. Walking briskly though aimlessly, since he is in a place he has never been, and avoiding strangers, he comes at last to a deserted part of town, tall buildings with bricked-up windows and what he takes to be the rigging of ships. With his brain roaring, he sits for a time with his hands over his ears and his feet in the gutter, all the inside of his head a blaze of red; then crawls into a doorway to sleep.

Once, in the night, a fierce-eyed little ragman comes, and takes him by the collar, and tries to push him into a sack. He breaks away, climbs a rope, tumbles into a box, and falls dead asleep.

When he wakes cold sunlight is on his cheek. The box has no lid. But he lies very still as he usually does in this particular dream and waits for Willett to find him: 'Ah, so that's where you've got to.'

But it isn't Willett. It is a big, tow-headed fellow of eighteen or nineteen, in a blue knitted cap and with dirty stubble on his cheek and no teeth, who hauls him up by the scruff of his neck so that he hangs like a rabbit outside a poulterer's shop. The youth's nose is on a level with his own; his legs are dangling. Then the mouth opens: 'Captain!' it bellows.

He had not meant to set himself loose in the world. He had not meant to end anything. He felt himself swinging now where the blue-capped youth held him in his fist, first one way, then another, and what he saw over the youth's shoulder terrified him: no gas-lamps, no houses, but a vastness of an ashen grey colour crawling with smoke as if the whole world was burning behind him.

He would learn to live with this crawling emptiness, but the first glimpse of it made his belly squirm. He had cast himself loose and the world had run away with him; he was lost, he was dangling, and would remain so till Willett, in an odour of char, with his eyebrows ablaze and his scorched boots hanging from their laces at his neck, turned up again to curse and wallop him, then, with a growl, take him back. He never ceased to expect that event and to fear it. He expected it still. A world from which Willett had entirely disappeared was inconceivable to him.

Willett's boots had reappeared: utterly real to him, every crack in their leather running with flame, the laces trailing, the tongue-flaps loose. It was Willett he could not find, though he heard him often enough, grumbling in the corners of the room, and smelt him there, a mixture of char and sweat, then at last the garden smell. He lay with his eyes closed, hands folded on his chest, his cheeks in the hot dark wet with tears. 'Ah, boy, so that's where you've got to!'

Where? Where had he got to?

Two years he was at sea. Or three. On one ship, then another: *The Gannet*, *The Star of Newcastle*, *The Charleston* – those were some of the names; last of all *The Pamukale*.

He made himself small, had a full belly, was often bullied and worse by the others. Mosey. The Irish.

Old Crouch, *The Pamukale*'s carpenter, was a good 'un. He liked to sing hymns while he worked and had two daughters, one a seal – a silkie he called her; she could change herself into a seal. He learned to use a chisel, a plane, a spirit level. Then, one day, too ill to care what happened to him and with no knowledge of what part of the world he was in – how would Willett find him here? – they put him overboard; he moved out of the shadow of the ship that tilted and creaked above him, out of its coolness, away from the faces at the rails. Burning alive down there, he felt the sun leap out, a single flame. All he had known shrank to a black dot jigging in his skull.

These visions that dragged him back and racked his body with the reliving of what he had already endured a first time, left him weak and shaken. Despite the kindness Mrs Hutchence showed him, and Leona's many attentions, he grew heartsick for his lean-to at the McIvors', and for the children, especially Lachlan. Meg and Janet he also missed, though he saw them almost daily. At Mrs Hutchence's they were absorbed now in a new life, the group round the kitchen table, where the presence of Hector and the schoolmaster, and the rapid talk, and so much laughter and play, confused him, kept him off. He began to sicken, and saw at last that what he was suffering here had to do with the sheets of paper where, months ago, Mr Frazer and the schoolmaster had set down his life. It was from there that the events of his former existence came and demanded to be turned back again from magic squiggles into the pain, joy, grief he was torn by, and which his present body was too weak to endure.

More and more now he was haunted by those sheets, seven in all, he had not forgotten the number, that Mr Frazer had folded and put into his pocket, and which he had never seen again; till he was convinced that the only way to save himself from so much racking, and despair and sweat, was to get them back again. They would be in one place or the other, those sheets; either at Mr Frazer's or at the school-house. All he needed was the strength to get there. But that was just what their magic had drawn from him.

17

WHEN LACHLAN BEATTIE looked about, it seemed to him that his whole world had come apart. The group of younger boys he moved among was all edge and shove. Their code was the same one their fathers used, but their fathers had seen enough of others' and their own deficiencies to draw back from unyielding absolutes. They could not. Lachlan, though he was smaller than the rest, had till now held authority over them and commanded fellows like Jeff Murcutt and the younger Corcorans. They saw their chance now and were after him.

He had always been a firebrand. When he first came among them it had amused the older fellows to taunt him. At the least touch he would fly red-faced to the attack. The others would strike back, but in a lazy fashion, condescendingly, since they were so much older. 'Lay off,' they would drawl, 'you mad bugger!' Very fast on his feet, he would duck in under their fists and leave them winded. They learned then. 'Honest, Locky,' Hec Gosper would tell him as they started off home, 'you're bloody mad!'

Hector, in those days, had not yet moved up into the group of older fellows, young men almost, who hung about the verandah of the store. Though convention decreed that he should ignore a mere ten-year-old so long as they were in company, Hector had from the beginning taken the younger boy under his wing. Lachlan, who was unhappy in the new place, was grateful for it, but wary too, at first. His accent was the point on which he was tormented, and he was concerned that what Hector might have in mind was a shared impediment.

It was a mean thought, and when he saw, as he did almost immediately, how open Hector was, how little of his own indirectness there was in the other boy, he was ashamed. There was always this seed of self-consciousness in him that made him suspicious and spoiled things. He grew fond of Hector and depended on him, so it was distressing when Gemmy's coming raised a conflict between them.

For the others, taunting Gemmy had become a new way – the old one had become stale by now – of provoking him, a new form of fun. These were the days when Gemmy was always at his heel, and he, still full of his moment at the fence, tended to swagger and show him off.

Hector did not join in these boyish scrabblings in the dust, he was too old for that; but he too was under the influence of that first day, and so long as others were about, kept up his grudge. It had put Lachlan in a spot. It was a matter of honour with him to stand up for Gemmy whatever the cost. He ignored Hector's gibes as long as he could, but the time came at last when he had to protest.

It was foolish of him. There were too many interested bystanders. Hector, furious that he had broken what he had thought was an understanding between them, could do nothing but respond. 'What?' he shouted. 'What's that?', and there was, on the first sound, as it burst from him, a little hissing through the nose that was the last of a defect he had eliminated save when he was out of control.

Lachlan was stricken. He would have given anything not to be the occasion of such a lapse. 'Com' awn, Gemmy,' he said and walked away, but the damage was done. There was, after that, an embarrassment between them that made it necessary, so long as others were about, to keep up a show

157

of hostility that each knew was a pretence. When they were not observed they fell back into their old intimacy, though it was constrained. On these occasions, Gemmy, who did not understand the rules they followed, was puzzled, and hurt too at times, by an inconsistency in Lachlan that he could not account for.

But Hector, at last, dropped out of the group of younger boys, keeping with fellows now who were his own age. Lachlan, not quite thirteen, was in between. He would leave school at Christmas, be free at last of the indignity of ink-stains on his fingers and the company of kids like Jeff Murcutt and the Corcorans, and littlies, and girls. In the meantime he began to test his welcome among the group at the store; he developed a talent for launching gobs of spit further than any of his fellows, laughed louder than the loudest of them at any sort of raw joke, and smoked and swore.

It was one of the conditions of his move into an older group that Gemmy could not appear, and he had, gently at first, then coldly, to discourage him. He was sorry for it. But it was absurd to have Gemmy always tagging at his heels, and he blushed now to recall a time when he had regarded it as a sign of his power. How puffed up he had been with his own importance! What a fool he must have appeared to the very fellows he had meant to impress!

His enlightenment had begun with the humiliations the schoolmaster had heaped upon him, and though he did not thank the man for it, he saw now that having set his face in the direction of manhood, he could not turn back. What he distrusted in himself was a tendency, a girlish one he thought, to let his affections rule. It was a weakness he was determined to stamp out. Still, there were days when he could not bear the look Gemmy wore, and would have given anything to step back a year and tell him, 'A'richt, Gemmy, com' awn then' – but what good would it do?

*

It was about the time of Gemmy's visit from the blacks and the series of accidents that had begun with the broken fence. Christmas was two months off. He was in the playground with companions he had outgrown.

'So where's yer mate,' Jeff Murcutt asked, 'yer shadow?' And then, looking about with mock surprise, 'Oh, I didn't see 'im!' Leo Corcoran had begun a little lopsided walk around them, with an expression so like Gemmy's that three or four younger boys, who were watching, rolled about in the dirt at such a show of brilliance.

'Shut your jaw,' Lachlan hissed.

'An' if I don't?'

Lachlan began to walk away.

'An' if I don't? What'll you do, eh? Get Gemmy t' set 'is blacks on us?'

He turned at that.

'You should hear what my Pa says. It's a wonder someone don't do the right thing, one a' these nights, and pot the bastard!'

Leo at that began his lopsided walk again, and Jeff Murcutt, with a grin, brought his arm up like a shotgun and followed Leo round the circle. There was a breathless moment in which boys of ten, eleven, some of them almost thirteen as Lachlan was, were soul-struck as he himself had been, that first day at the fence, by the evocation of arms. Jeff Murcutt stood empowered in the midst of them, actually changed, himself impressed almost to awe by what he was reaching for, and Leo hovered. Then Jeff's lips moved. 'Bang!' he said, not loud.

The puff of air out of his mouth struck Leo in the chest. He hung in the air, mouth open, head thrown back, one hand at his breast, and they watched him, slowly, buckle at the knees and fall.

It was in the same playground circle, two days later, that he heard of the night attack.

He had known at breakfast that something was amiss but nothing was said, and it was a sign of how things had changed among them that he dared not ask. His aunt fussed and looked strained, his uncle was soft with him. He kept looking from one to the other waiting for enlightenment.

'I hear you had a bit of strife last night,' Jeff Murcutt announced. The others looked interested; they knew no more, Lachlan saw, than he did. He narrowed his eyes and did not respond, but felt his heart knock against his ribcage and knew, from the sudden dizziness he felt, that he had gone pale. Let Jeff Murcutt tell, if he knew something. But all he did was stand smirking, with his head down and his toes scuffing the dust.

It was Jed Corcoran, poor dumb Jed, who did the asking. He thought he was the only one who did not know.

'What strife? What happened?' he said in his babyish, snot-thickened voice.

'*He* knows,' Jeff Murcutt told him.

Jed Corcoran turned his soft eyes on him. 'What Locky? What happened?'

Lachlan turned and strode away. 'What?' he heard Jed ask again. 'I din' hear nothing.'

He felt betrayed on all sides. That Janet had been there, and he had not. That he had slept through it like a mere kid. That they had let him sleep, as if he could be no help, and had afterwards kept it from him!

It was his aunt who told him the details at last, white-faced, taut as a wire, speaking through clenched lips. He understood how his uncle felt because he too felt the power drain from him and the stab of fear; not at what he might have to face – he would face anything, he was brave enough – but at what he might have to admit of the way the world was, and how his failure to see it was a weakness in him.

He did not go to school. He took his gun and went off into the bush, but all he did was sit, hunched up with the

160

gun in his lap, trying to see how they could go on now, how their life, his life, could ever be settled and ordinary again.

It was out here that Hector found him.

'Wha' do *you* want?' he called.

Hector, a little way off, squatted on his heels. He plucked a grass-stalk and put it between his crooked teeth.

'Well?' Lachlan demanded. He had to fight to keep back tears.

Hector continued to sit, his hat down over his eyes, the lip showing clear under his pale moustache.

He knew what Hector was doing. He had decided to sit, saying nothing, since there was nothing words could say, and wear him down. And it happened. The hostility he felt melted in him, and after a little, still without speaking, Hector got to his feet and walked away.

With Gemmy's removal to a distance a kind of normality did come back to them in a pretence on all sides that what had occurred was a misunderstanding and no harm done.

His aunt, always a realist, went along with it. When her neighbours turned up, full of high spirits, to gossip or bring recipes or ask for help with a bit of sewing, she welcomed them, frostily at first, and never quite in the old way; she had a kind of reserve now that would never leave her. They knew it and took her as she was.

Things were not so easy for his uncle. Lachlan saw this because he too felt it. Something had been destroyed in him that could not be put right. He watched his uncle drift back after a time to his friends, to Barney Mason, Jim Sweetman, but the days of unselfconscious trust in his standing among them, and the belief that to be thought well of by such fellows was the first thing in the world, were gone. He was watchful now. There was always a little niggling worm of denial in him, a need to seek out, even in the straightest of men, some hint of crookedness that might be the truth even they did not know. He was quieter these days. He had moved away into a distance in himself that even Lachlan felt he could not presume on, and what he experienced there began to engrave itself in lines upon him, though he too kept up the pretence that life, in something like the old form, had resumed and would go on.

Lachlan did not believe it. He was still at the stage where everything presented itself in the absolute, as a possibility to be carried blithely into the future or done with, once and for all. When he was forced to qualify, as with Hector, he felt uneasy. He was so changeable himself he wanted the world, even in the bitter form in which he now saw it, to be fixed. So when he went to visit Gemmy at Mrs Hutchence's, a little shamefaced at having left it so long, he was surprised to walk in on a noisy company whose existence he had had no conception of, though Janet, and Meg too, had tried to tell him of it. And here they were, all, seated at a table among teacups and crumbs – Janet, Meg, Gemmy, Hector, even the schoolmaster – with Leona pouring tea out of a blue pot. They turned to face him, looking up out of the same mid-sentence, whose unfinished hilarity hung in the air, and he saw with a pang that in all these last weeks, which had been such misery to him, they had been happily settled, even Hector, in this lighted corner of the world.

They made a place for him. Leona introduced herself, and gave him tea. There was a little cake too, with raisins in it, which crumbled in his hand when he bit into it. He looked up, very self-conscious, to see if it mattered, but it appeared not to, and he added to the scatter of crumbs.

Just the same, he felt awkward. They went back to their lively chatter, which was all half-joking banter that the others seemed practised in and which he did not know how to enter; all its terms were unfamiliar to him. He sat glum

162

and silent and only Gemmy, he thought, amid so much jollity, moved in the same dark strand with him.

But he felt displeased with himself. There was, he saw, some other lighter way of responding to things. These others had found it. What was wrong with him that he could not?

He kept an eye on Hector. He had expected the older boy might be abashed at being caught like this in the company of women, and girls – not to speak of the schoolmaster. He kept waiting for Hector to tip him off, with a wink, that his part in it was a kind of foolery. But Hector was the noisiest among them. Didn't he know what a clown he was making of himself, with his slick hair and his empty gallantries, or that Leona, to whom they were addressed, made fun of them and was too old for him? He blushed for his friend. Only slowly did it occur to him that some of Hector's showing off was for his benefit; he was expected to be impressed.

What puzzled him most was the presence of the school-master, who said very little. Was he embarrassed at being discovered here, as Hector might have been and was not? But after a little he saw that Mr Abbot too was included in Leona's teasing, and did not mind it any more than Hector did, and that Hector's sallies, in a joking way that suggested an understanding between them, were meant to be measured against what Mr Abbot could produce.

He produced very little. It was Hector who set the pace – Lachlan was astonished, where had he learned all this? – and was the more unconstrained, the more skilled too, at answering Leona back and provoking and pleasing her.

She tried the game, briefly, with him. She had a different tone for each of them, and he thought he detected in the one she chose for him a degree of mockery – for his youth, was it? – that brought a flush of indignation to his cheek. She saw it and drew back, but when he was ignored he took offence. She saw that too, but did not know how to help him.

And Janet?

In these last months they had grown apart. He was already aware of a change in her, but it was now, in this company, that he saw how great it might be. He had taken for granted always that their lives were intertwined, by which he meant that her chief concern must be him. She did nothing to deny it, but was absorbed, he saw, in a world of her own that he had no part in. He caught looks between her and his aunt that had not been there before, and when he burst in upon them once, with his usual expectation of welcome, was surprised by the faces they turned to him, which were attentive but subtly closed.

It had struck him then, and for the first time, that there might be areas of experience that he was not intended to enter. That closed look marked only the closest and most gently guarded of them. Beyond lay others that had never heard of him and never would hear.

He was shaken. In the revelation that a power he had taken for granted in himself might have limitations, he felt much of it fall away.

Meanwhile, here at the table, Janet met his eyes and flushed with embarrassment. Not surely for him!

He found an excuse to get away, though Leona protested. Gemmy went with him, and they walked a little way on the road together. They barely spoke. Gemmy was sick. He too felt sick at heart. He promised to return but knew that he would not, and Gemmy knew it too. They stood a moment, then he turned and moved away.

He looked back once and saw that Gemmy too had turned, about sixty yards off, and they faced one another down the white ribbon of track. They were too far off to be more to one another than figures whose eyes, whose real dimensions even, were lost to distance.

For years afterwards he would have dreams in which he would stand trying, against the fact of distance, to see the look on Gemmy's face, and once or twice, in his dream, he walked back through the white dust, which rose in ghostly spirals around him, and went right up to where he was standing, and looked into his face. But it remained as blurred as it had been from sixty yards off, and he woke with his cheeks wet, even after so long, though he was no longer a child.

18

AFTER THREE YEARS in the north, Mr Frazer was delighted with Brisbane. The service at Marr's Boarding House was cheerful, the jug and basin on the washstand a wonderful guarantee of the amenities, clear water, steaming hot in the mornings, and the soup at the *table d'hôte* agreeably thick.

The little town was very little, not much more really than a village, and this surprised him considering the almost mystical importance they attached to it 'up there', but impressive monuments were in sight. They were shadowy as yet behind scaffolding, but one or two of them had stepped clear and stood broad-fronted and substantial above the verandahed hotels and weatherboard bank buildings and stores, the picket fences, and rutted, rather twisty lanes where, on his morning walk to the top of a wooded ridge, he met barefooted youths driving cows.

The Governor, he soon discovered, was a very visible figure. He dashed about the unpaved streets in a gleaming chariot, wearing epaulettes and a sword, and gave the impression, with his ramrod stance and lean profile, of being the embodiment of a distant, almost unapproachable power. But when Mr Frazer presented himself at Government House, it was Sir George himself who looked out of a window and called him in.

It was as if he had arrived at a rundown country mansion, Palladian in style but with household arrangements that appeared to be Irish, or perhaps the climate had something to do with it; the day was sultry. Toys and flowers with their heads off lay scattered about the entrance hall, which otherwise was very empty – a child's hobbyhorse, several wooden animals. There were scurryings in side rooms and a woman's voice raised in complaint.

Sir George came out and seemed irritated by the commotion. Ignoring Mr Frazer and the startled footman, he flung open a door, stood glaring, and the scufflings ceased; but his face, when he turned, remained peevish, and Mr Frazer had the impression, a flash, no more, not of a naval man retired early but of a dignified upper servant who had been caught in his master's clothes and was convinced, if he was overbearing enough, that he would get away with it. 'My dear fellow,' he exclaimed, with sudden affability, 'do come in. I'm delighted.'

The interview that followed was a puzzle to Mr Frazer. He felt that he had never quite got the hang of it, or of Sir George either.

Sir George, having recovered his poise, appeared a fine, bluff fellow, not so old as you might have thought, and not at all stiff; he invited you to be entirely open with him. But Mr Frazer was disconcerted, just the same, by the line of questioning he took. He had written earlier, no doubt, to Mr Herbert – it was Mr Herbert who had set him on to make this *report*? No? Then it was one or other of the people up there (the Governor pushed about a pile of papers he had before him and seemed more and more put out) whom of course he had complete knowledge of – Mr McIntosh, perhaps, one of the O'Hares? It occurred to Mr Frazer after a moment that he was suspected of being an emissary, a secret one, though Sir George had nosed him out, of forces that Sir George was at war with, and who were always, by one means or another, trying to get under his guard. Sir George fixed him with a hurt look, accusatory blue. Am I right sir? Have I found you out?

Not at all, he insisted. He had come here entirely in his own right, on behalf – very briefly, though he feared not briefly enough, he tried to describe Gemmy, who was not very easily describable; how the man, through his knowledge of native life, had led him etc . . . It was enough anyway to satisfy Sir George that he was not one of a cabal, yet another subverter of the great design, and that his report was not part of a plan to entrap and discredit him.

But once the report was rendered harmless Sir George lost interest in it, and in Gemmy too. 'Yes, yes,' he muttered, 'an interesting case – they are interesting people – ' but a moment later they had leapt to Hesiod and arrived, before Mr Frazer had quite caught up, at Homer, a frequent destination, he guessed, in Sir George's conversational flights.

Sir George's commission here is to call into existence a new self-governing state; in a land, territory rather, about the size of France and all the Germanies combined, wild, cut in two by the southern tropic, and largely, as yet, unpeopled. He is alternately intoxicated by the largeness of the undertaking and depressed that in being set down, at more than forty, at the ends of the earth, he may drop from sight. To keep his name before the Lords in Westminster he writes to one or another of them almost daily, describing in grandiloquent terms, all classical allusion and analogy, the names he has bestowed on a nameless part of the empire, the towns he has founded, the laws laid down. He sees himself as a kind of imperial demiurge, out of mere rocks and air creating spaces where history may now occur – at once the Hesiod of the place, its Solon, and its antipodean Pericles.

The archaic and the classical, indeed the prehistoric and the classical, exist side by side here and in the same moment. Sir George finds it entirely understandable that in the little coastal port he has honoured with his name a crocodile has been seen to emerge from the mud and waddle unperturbed about the main street, and that in his capital of a mere five thousand souls the monuments he is building, dome and portico, rise in incongruous glory above the backs of bullock teams, the curses of their drivers, and under the gaze of creatures, only recently redeemed from nakedness, whose minds are still sunk in unfathomable night.

They are in the age of wonders here, where forms, nameless as yet, are just beginning to emerge out of the dark, the dreamlike: the age of the hippogriff and demigorgon, of the heroes and demigods, too, of future legend, who just happen to have names like Jones and Dalrymple, and wear moleskins, or, as he does, the uniform of Her Majesty's Colonial Service. 'Your town,' he writes to his patron, Lord Cardwell, of the little mosquito-infested port in the north on which he has settled that great man's name, 'lies in a position analogous to that of Thermopylae; that is, at the north end of the Australian Epirus'. In his mind, as it soars and hangs eagle-like over the great expanse of past and future, the local squattocracy, rough fellows most of them, are his squatter kings. 'Runs (the colonial term for a wide-ranging pasture)' he informs one of his Lordships, 'seems a literal translation of δρόμοι εὐρέες of Homer, where the shepherd kings feed their cattle in a similar climate to that of Arcadia. How refreshing among my daily cares are these classical analogies.' Being escorted into a little western town of nine pubs and a butcher shop, by a party of two hundred stockmen, he sees himself riding in the company of attendant centaurs. Analogy is his drug. He finds it everywhere.

At eighteen he fell in love with the Mediterranean. Twenty years later he married into it. Lady Bowen, Roma Diamantina, is the daughter of the President of the Senate of Corfu, the Count Candiano di Roma.

Queensland, one has to say, was not Sir George's first choice, but he is determined to make the most of it. He refuses to be put off by its failure at times to come up to the mark. His own mind knows no bounds. He is monstrously ambitious. What he fears is that if he is too successful here he will be taken for granted and overlooked; but there are occasions when he fears even more that he may be *exposed*, since the secret that gnaws his soul, child as he is of a Donegal rectory, is that he is an imposter.

Sir George, easy now, reaches behind him and slips from a shelf two little volumes of which he is himself the very modest author. Mr Frazer is impressed.

One is an argument in favour of the present island of Ithaca as the site of Homer's island; the other an account of a journey on horseback, across Thessaly and the High Pindus, from Constantinople to Corfu. Sir George, it appears, has stood at the summit of all three classical peaks, Etna, Parnassus, Mount Olympus – a feat no other Briton has emulated. But when he opens the atlas he has recently commissioned, and they look together at the town there that bears Sir George's name, Mr Frazer, remembering the scattered huts along the shore and the listless air about the jetty he sailed from, for he knows the actual place, feels his confidence in the Governor take a downward turn. A kind of gloom comes over him. Sir George, he decides, exudes an air of magnificent unreality that includes everything he looks upon. He has got close enough to feel its disintegrating effect in every part of him.

They do come back to his report, Sir George *has* read it. Perhaps now, Mr Frazer thinks, taking a firm hold on his own sinking spirits, we will get down to facts. In all this heady leaping about the globe he had grown more and more conscious of Gemmy, poor fellow; so real in the room that he can almost smell him, and, in a malicious moment, wishes Sir George could too.

But Sir George has no interest in facts. He takes the long view, the long *high* view, and from there, since his mind has the same capacity to leap centuries into the future as back into the past, the whole of time being its sphere, the vision Mr Frazer has outlined in his report of orchards, not of exotic (that is, European) but of native fruit, stretching in all directions to the skyline, had long since passed the arguing and planning stage, the clearing and grafting and seed-and-sapling stage, and is, in Sir George's mind, accomplished. To descend to detail would be to miss the wood for the scrubby little trees. That sort of thing he leaves to those who have a talent for it, who love to burrow and bury themselves (he is glaring again) in minutiae, dull fellows, dull facts. Recovering quickly, he beams at Mr Frazer, whom he sees as a man, after all, consumed by an idea, with no one behind him, a man he can trust. He expresses his entire satisfaction with their little talk and invites him to dinner where he will have the pleasure (Sir George looks humorous) of meeting the Premier, Mr Herbert – and Lady Bowen, of course. Thursday then, seven sharp.

But at this descent to mere detail Sir George grows gloomy again, suspicious – or perhaps a new barb has found its mark and is working its slow poison in him. When Mr Frazer gets up to leave he has set his jaw and is gazing irascibly out the window towards the dispiriting bushland of the opposing shore.

Two nights later, in the prettily furnished dining room at Government House, they are four at table: Sir George; Lady Bowen, a fine, tall, dark-haired woman, not quite beautiful but with splendid shoulders and eyes; Mr Frazer himself; and the Premier, Mr Herbert, a very young man with soft fair hair and a large head, who has walked in the three miles from Herston, his estate on the edge of town, with his dog, Skip, and a basket of fresh vegetables.

171

Mr Herbert lives at Herston with his friend of Oxford days, Mr Bramston. The house, with its animals and its model garden, is a joint enterprise, as is suggested by the merging of the young men's names – a Horatian retreat for Mr Herbert from the rough and tumble of colonial democracy, which he does not believe in, and the game, which does not quite suit him, of state-making.

Mr Herbert, the only son of the fifth son of an Earl, is in all ways the gentleman amateur, but one, Sir George finds, who has set out, almost in the spirit of contradiction, to be rigorously professional in everything he does. It is a matter of character. He is painstaking, dedicated, self-effacing and smug – this is Sir George's view, who suspects him, correctly as it happens, of reporting unfavourably upon him to his great family at home.

Mr Herbert, who has a good deal to put up with, regards Sir George as a madman, but one he has a kind of responsibility for: an autocratic, impulsive, obstinate, ceremoniously pedantic, fantastical, profoundly humourless man with only one gift, a strong but inconvenient memory, which nature has bestowed upon him in compensation, it would appear, for his entire lack of sense.

The two men are as different as they can be.

Sir George is hungry for office and has a premonition already that the higher forms of it will elude him; not, he believes, through any fault of his own but through neglect, not to say malice, at home.

Mr Herbert is made for success but winces at it. He does not despise office, even high office, but his austere nature and distaste for every sort of public display means that he would prefer it to be anonymous; what his soul craves is privacy. He is weary of his term here, which he looks upon already as an adventure of his youth. He is weary of Sir George and his infantile vanities and *crises ministérielles*. He is even weary, at times, of the little boat in which, since he is fond of the outdoors and all manly pursuits, he likes to skip about on the waters of the bay, and of Herston, the fifty acres of Cambridgeshire he has established in a place that, once he leaves it, he will not revisit. All of which, and more, is in the air as the servants move behind them at table.

Mr Frazer has the sense of being an intruder here among people who have been too long shut up together, have already said everything they can bear to say to one another and are speaking in code.

'Really, Mr Frazer,' says Lady Bowen, 'you should see Herston.' (They are eating some of the Herston vegetables, so the subject has arisen quite naturally.) 'You would think yourself in England. The peaches! So plump, and with such a blush on the skin. Even at Corfu we had nothing like them. We are very gay when we go to Herston. Mr Herbert has a machine for making ice brought all the way from India, from which he makes, with his own hands – ' the word, on the lady's breath, hangs a little, so that Mr Frazer is aware of the knuckles in young Mr Herbert's broad hands as he works his knife and fork – 'the most delicious water-ice. The children are very fond of water-ice. Especially little George.'

'Our asparagus, this year,' Mr Herbert announces at another point, and the colour comes to his cheek, 'is quite special. People told us, you know, that it couldn't be done. Too damp. But there it is.'

'And the strawberries,' says Lady Bowen, darting a quick glance at Sir George who has put his knife and fork down, drawn himself up and is smouldering. 'The children had never seen strawberries – actually *growing*. Peeping out under their little – leaves.'

This talk of fruit and vegetables, especially in the tension it seems to create, unnerves Mr Frazer. It is intended, he believes, to make way for his report. He waits for Sir George now to take up what Lady Bowen has so skillfully prepared, and wonders when he does not if *he* should do it. Surely not. Then it occurs to him that he has mistaken things altogether. Sir George finds this talk of gardens and strawberries and asparagus suspicious, sinister even – is that it? A way of informing him, indirectly (in which case it would be Mr Herbert's business Lady Bowen has been doing), that his interest in the native fruit scheme is known and that if he wants to save himself from absolute folly, he had better pull out while he can. Sir George's anxiety, Mr Frazer sees, is that he may speak out and embarrass him.

So the litany of Herston's splendours goes on from grapes and China peaches to its mouse deer, its Breton cows, its Arabian bull, its peacocks, pheasants, guinea pigs, and, after a strained half hour of port, they retire at last to the sitting room. Here Lady Bowen, in a sweet Italian voice and with a delicate touch on the keys, sings from the sheet music Mr Herbert has brought, while Skip, at his master's feet, looks on, and coffee is brought, and they settle into a cosy torpor in which Mr Frazer fears he may doze off.

Suddenly there is an explosion in the room. Lady Bowen has slapped her forearm. A smudge of crimson appears there, the rich blood of the Candianos, which she stares at a moment – they all do – as if she had not expected it to be quite so scarlet or so abundant. She rises and leaves the room.

Clouds of mosquitos have drifted in from the mangroves downriver – the price of the cooling breeze that has sprung up – and go sailing by with their fine legs hanging. When Lady Bowen returns the blood is gone and she has a servant with her who bears in each hand a lighted coil of some sharp smelling stuff (dried cow-manure, Mr Frazer guesses) that he sets on the floor, and from which thin smoke weaves upward and spreads.

From Sir George's reproachful look as he takes his leave, Mr Frazer guesses that he has in some way offended. He has failed to play some role he was assigned here, which he was not clever enough, or socially adroit enough, to perceive. Or he has been too responsive to Mr Herbert; whom he finds rather attractive on the whole, very manly and unassuming and, at one moment, when he took the opportunity, perhaps foolishly, to speak of Gemmy – whose name Mr Herbert already knew – very attentive and sympathetic. Sir George has seen it and sniffed out a defection, a choice of loyalties. Anyway, next morning, at Marr's, there is a note.

It is from the Premier and is in two parts. The first thanks him, mysteriously, for his 'understanding' on the previous evening. 'I was – I presume here on your confidence – very grateful for that, as I daresay was our hostess, though I speak, of course, only for myself . . .'

And the second?

'I have, after our brief conversation, been considering what might be done for Mr Fairley, whose position, I believe, was your chief reason for coming to us. I have pleasure in inform-ing you that I have arranged for him to be offered the post of Customs Officer at the port of Bowen, at a salary of fifty pounds per annum, the official notification of which, etc, etc.'

He was astonished. Had he made himself so unclear? Was it a return for his 'understanding' of a situation he had not understood? Was it a joke whose humour he was expected to recognise – at the expense, perhaps, of Sir George? Was it cynicism? Was it large-handed indifference? Anyway, it was what he took back with him.

The orchards he had foreseen receded into a future that appeared increasingly remote but no more unreal to him than the place he now stood in, with the Premier's letter in his hand, the jug and basin with their nasturtium pattern, sitting solidly on the washstand, and the busy little capital coming to life beyond the sill, all its picket fences gleaming, the relentless sunlight bouncing off its domes.

19

A DAY OF BUSHFIRES, brassy sky; the air stilled, smelling of char. Fine ash falling, as if the sun at last had
burnt itself out and the last flakes of it were descending to
cover the earth. It did not surprise him. He too felt burnt
out, his skull a husk, paper-thin and rattling as he walked.
He felt, as he followed the white ribbon that led to the
settlement, that he had lost all weight in the world; his feet
made so little impression in the dust that it was as if he had
not passed, or had passed through into another being and
no longer shared – with the powdery dust under his feet, the
rocks, the trees along the way where he paused a moment
to rest, and settling his palm against a tree trunk, felt the
sap streaming up from where the giant tree was rooted – the
hold these things had on the earth. He shuffled. He tottered.
His tongue felt brittle in his mouth as an insect's wing. He
was going to claim back his life; to find the sheets of paper
where all that had happened to him had been set down in
the black blood that had so much power over his own: the
events, things, people too, that sprang to life in them, Willett's boots, the ferrets, Mosey and The Irish. Magicked into
squiggles, like the ghosts of insects under bark, they had
drawn the last of his spirit from him. They were drawing
him to his death.

George Abbot, at his desk in the schoolroom, had a pile of

papers before him and a pen in his hand. More lives, Gemmy thought, that out there somewhere held others in their spell.

He seemed a different figure, this man in his shirtsleeves with his shirt open and the pen in his hand, from the youth he sometimes saw at the kitchen table. He was in his role here of sorcerer. He felt the power of that in him even at Mrs Hutchence's, where he was called George. He was not what he seemed.

He recalled the old harshness with which, in the days when he had followed Lachlan and the girls to school, the man had driven him away. He had smelled on him then an aversion that came from the blood, and was not convinced by the familiarity he had begun to show him or the attempts he made at kindness. It was not done for his benefit – or so he thought – but to impress Leona.

A man may have two natures. Here at his desk the school-teacher was in the other darker and more powerful one, seated before a pile of papers, with at his elbow the bottle with the spirit that smelled of earth.

George Abbot, looking up from his tedious corrections, was surprised to see Gemmy at the window. He was startled. How long had he been there? He felt a kind of goosepimpling at the intensity of his look. The fellow seemed sick, out of himself. He got up quickly and helped him in.

It took him a little time to understand what he wanted. His garbled speech, all stutters, made no sense, and he thought at first he must be delirious. He was asking for people George had never heard of, or so he thought, till one name, Willett, struck him, and he remembered some bit of what, nearly a year ago, he had set down, and in this very room too. It was then that he grasped it. He wanted *that* – that piece of writing. He wanted it back. Well he did not have it, of course. Mr Frazer did. Mr Frazer was in Brisbane.

'This, Gemmy?' he asked, holding up one of the exercises he had been correcting.

Gemmy, looking rather sly, reached out and, not quite grasping, relieved him of it. George was surprised at himself. At the ease with which he let it go.

Gemmy raised the sheet to his nostrils and sniffed, and a look George Abbot could not have defined, but would never forget, spread over his features. He waited in expectation, and George, more out of curiosity than anything else, or to see the look again, offered him a second sheet, then another, till seven of the ill-written exercises, all blotches and scratchings out, had passed from his hand to Gemmy's.

'What do you want them for?' he asked.

Gemmy looked at him gravely and did not reply. He slipped the papers into his pocket and George, inwardly, shrugged. Useless, he decided, to demand them back.

'You should go home now, Gemmy,' he said gently. 'They'll be worrying about you. Do you want me to come with you?'

He shook his head, and began, alarmed perhaps, to get up, but tottered.

'Here, let me get you something,' he said. 'A slice of bread – some water.'

The man sat again and he went quickly into the little room behind the blackboard and cut a thick slice of bread, poured a mug of water. He was only gone a moment. But when he came back to the schoolroom, with the plate in one hand and the mug in the other, Gemmy was gone. Puzzled, he set the bread and water down, and went back to his corrections – or what remained of them. What would he tell Jeff Murcutt and the rest, whose exercises, sweated over in the narrow desks, turned this way and that to get a better purchase on the paper, grimed with dirt, smeared with ink, filled painfully with what he had knocked into their skulls, he had allowed Gemmy – just like that – to walk off with.

Since he had begun to love but also to forget himself a little, the world and everything around him appeared in a new light. He regarded Gemmy very differently now from when he had sat at the table here, an unwilling schoolboy, and taken down the 'facts' Mr Frazer dictated. Gemmy had repelled him then. Something in the muddiness of his eye, the meaty stench he gave off, a filth, ingrained, ineradicable perhaps – most of all in his cringing eagerness to please, had challenged his belief that suffering, even of the most degrading sort, would bring out the best in a man, and that the spectacle of it must inspire noble sentiments. Well, no noble sentiments had come to him when he was faced with Gemmy. If what had survived in this brutish specimen was, as Mr Frazer appeared to believe, naked essential humanity, then it was too little. He held his nose. He wanted no part of it. What a high-minded, fastidious little theorist he had been. Was youth an excuse? Unhappiness? He no longer thought so.

Part of the affront he had felt as Mr Frazer agonised over the greasy rag of a man, who had never perhaps been more than a plain imbecile, was that in all the time he had been here, he had never once shown any feeling for *him*.

But there had been something deeper, even then. It was the fear that Mr Frazer, for all his embarrassing effusions, might be right. That what they were dealing with, in Gemmy, might be closer to them, to *him*, than he knew. Mr Frazer had accepted that from the start – he paid that much tribute to the man. He, choked by the stench of the suggestion, by what he felt as its blackening touch upon him, had fought it, but come round at last. He felt humbled now; and most of all when Gemmy, recalling no doubt the persecutions he had used against him, shrank at his approach. He saw – it was still himself he was thinking of, it was the only way he could grasp what others felt – that there might be something after all in mere endurance. He would have liked to break through the silence that kept Gemmy apart from them, find what it was in him that had made that possible, discover what had been done to him, beyond what was visible in the marks he bore, the one eyebrow that gave him his quizzical, wren-like look, that had harmed him in one part and in another had not, so that he had at moments, and most of all when he appeared merely dumb and ox-like, a kind of grandeur that went painfully to the heart.

'Grandeur' was the word that came to him, and he did not reject it. It did not seem too large for what he saw at times in a man who had been kicked from one side of the world to the other, not even knowing perhaps what part of it he was in, except that he was there in his own skin. That, the skin, is what he had come down to from the realm of noble sentiments.

They were in a place, a continent, where it was mere naked endurance perhaps that best revealed the qualities of men. And that might be true of every place, when the fabric of pageant and the illusion of noble sentiments had been ripped away. In any event, he cared enough for Gemmy now to lay his corrections aside and set off for Mrs Hutchence's, to see the fellow had got safely home. If he hurried, he thought, he might catch him up on the road.

Leaving the schoolhouse, Gemmy paused a moment, the papers safely in his pocket, and as he looked about him, felt for the first time that he could go any way he pleased; he did not have to go back down the ribbon of road.

To the north, beyond the swamp and its band of ti-tree forest, the sky was a smoky glow, cloudless because what filled it was a single cloud, blooming with a light that might have been that of the fallen sun, its ashes shaken out now and even the deep core failing. The forests up there had all day been climbing into the sky and drifting down again to cover all this side of the range with ash; a breath out of the heart of the country. There was no finality in it. He knew that. One life was burned up, hollowed out with flame, to crack the seeds from which new life would come; that was the law. The seasons here were fire, ash, then the explosion out of blackened earth and charred, unkillable stumps, of springy shoots and loose-folded, sticky little leaves; the hard seed tormented with flame till it splits, springs open, then a hissing as the first raindrops plump and spatter, and the new forest, leaf by leaf in its old shape, ghostly at first in its feathery lightness, breathes out of charred sticks and smoulder in a season too long to be measured by days or moons or by one man's life or many.

He walked swiftly now over the charred earth and was himself crumbling. If he did not find the word soon that would let him enter here, there would be nothing left of him but a ghost of heat, a whiff as he passed of fallen ash.

A drop of moisture sizzled on his tongue: the word – he had found it. *Water*. Slow dribbles of rain began to fall. He was entering rain country. Soon the sky let down tangled streamers, and he was walking now in a known landscape; all the names of things, as he met them, even in their ashen form, shone on his breath, sprang up in their real lives about him, succulent green, soft paw and eyeball, muscle tense under fur.

He still carried in his pocket the sheets of paper on which they had written down his life. He took them out now. They were sodden. Rain had begun to wash the writing from them, the names, the events; their black magic now a watery sky-colour, the sooty grains sluicing away even as he watched; the paper turning pulpy, beginning to break up in his hands, dropping like soggy crumbs from his fingers into puddles where he left them, bits all disconnected . . . *and my friens Billy an . . . pretty little black patch over . . . thunder Then . . . of every colour of . . .*

20

T HE SISTERS OF St Iona's, Wynnum, were in a state
of mild but pleasant ferment. The motor that emerged
between the rusty palms of their drive, with its gleaming
radiator grille and swoop of mudguards over spoked wheels,
was a novelty. Almost beautiful in its way, it nosed its metal
form, all purring, into the quiet of their walled retreat (the
walls were ten feet high, spiked at the top with shards of
glass from ginger beer and lemonade bottles), an impressive
but dangerous reminder of a world they had set themselves
apart from, though not entirely, and which had lately
become very noisy and tragically interesting. The driver too,
when he leapt out, was a novelty. That the occupant of the
car was less so did not spoil the effect.

The world *he* belonged to was familiar. It was that of
their fathers and brothers, the bushman in three-piece suit
down for The Show. He had none of the up-to-date glamour
of the driver, though he too, in fact, was an older man, and
drew what they saw in him of the brute world that began
at their gates from the animal sheen of his jacketed shoulders
and the polish on his boots. He moved round in front of his
machine and set his hand to chrome. The Minister's shaggy
head appeared. Manoeuvring his large frame out of the door,
he shook himself as it were on the path.

He was here to see their own Sister Monica, who had, in
these last weeks, done a quite extraordinary thing: she had
got herself into the papers.

Some of her letters had been intercepted by the authorities

and she had been suspected, briefly, of being a risk to security, perhaps a spy. It was nonsense of course and soon proved so; but some of the sisters had looked at her for a time with new eyes – the suspicion, after all, the mere possibility, was something – and one or two of them had been pleased to see her momentarily brought down. She was, to say no more, an infuriating woman, in no way humble; though they too, of course, were happy to have the cloud lifted from their little community, and the now famous correspondence declared innocuous, if not quite commonplace; unconnected, anyway, with news, battles, anger and the confirmation, unnecessary one might have thought, of dominion loyalty.

Still, they fluttered at the promise of yet another ministerial visitation. The *man* had not been cleared, or not in the public eye; and they rather enjoyed the hint, beyond his obvious plain looking and plain speaking, of something not quite trustworthy in him. It confirmed them in their distrust of the world, especially the active, overbearing male part of it. Some of them rushed about to see that the bannisters were without dust, rubbed their elbows on window-glass, peered at the tiles in the entry hall for heel-marks and scratches, as if he were here as an inspector of their devotion to the *domestic* virtues, to expose them as housewives largely failed. Discreetly, from upper windows, they watched Sister Monica, kilting her skirt up over her boots, go down the stone steps to greet him.

'Lachlan,' she said, and kissed him, first on one cheek then the other. 'Hello,' he replied, and glanced up under his brows at the watchers, who sprang back behind glass.

Even if no one could hear, he never quite knew how to address her in these moments when they were still in view. Later, she would be plain Janet. He could never quite come at 'Sister' or 'Monica'.

'Let's get away from the gallery,' she said.

'Forty minutes, Wilson,' he told the driver, who clicked

his heels; then, very aware of the impression he was making above, moved across to the lawn and stood, back to the building, legs apart, with the sun on his shoulders, a thin trail of smoke rising before him, and myna birds pecking boldly round his boots.

The convent was an imposing structure of sandstone and timber with a double-storeyed verandah, open below but with rust-stained venetians above. The roof was of colonial iron but the towers at either end, each with its set of louvred windows, and the columnated brick chimneys, gave it a baronial, almost Elizabethan look.

It had been built, with ballroom, billiard room and separate kitchen and servants' quarters, for a local shipping magnate, whose fortune, before Federation put an end to that sort of thing, had been based on blackbirding for the sugar interests up north. His widow, an organiser, these days, of charity balls for the War effort, had deeded it to the sisters, as part of a bid for respectability in which the family name, in keeping with the new mood of expeditionary fervour and heroic self-sacrifice, would be relieved of the stain of Early Days in the South Seas, and the old ruffian who had been the scourge of all the nearby islands could become, with his white waistcoat and whiskers, a benign, grandfatherly figure, the very embodiment of the last great, if rather rough age of hobnailed visionaries. In this form his portrait dominated the staircase with its cedar newel posts and spindles, glaring down in regret, perhaps, of the children and grandchildren he had expected to fill the house when he first conceived it in the loneliness of nights up in the tropics, or in disapproval of the women in sensible boots who crossed and recrossed the stained-glass entry hall with their hands in their pockets, or, with skirts hauled up in the freedom of seclusion, swabbed its tiles with lye.

On his first visit, Lachlan Beattie had been entertained by the Mother Superior. Passing under the gaze of the old cut-throat (he had come across Duncan McGregor once or twice in earlier days, an unedifying experience), he had been led into a dark, overfurnished room to sip tea from a little ladylike cup, while Janet, impatiently, looked on.

The Mother Superior was a sensible woman, not inclined to panic at their moment of notoriety. She had allowed him to charm her, as she had him, but did not see him again. These days, free of formality, Janet led him round past the shabby side of the building towards the garden.

Things were ramshackle back here. There were tubs and a blackened furnace for washdays, and down a path of uneven bricks, two lopsided dunnies under a crown of pink antignon. He imagined the sisters slopping out after dark under umbrellas in their loose boots, and the nightmen with cans on their shoulders, staggering to their wagons early enough on hot mornings not to cross one of the sisters on the path.

The garden, this afternoon, was steaming after a down-pour. Snails were out, dragging their shells from under cassia and canna bushes. Sister Monica, Janet, very deliberately set her boots down in a little crunching dance this way and that in front of him. He felt, as he passed, the drag of a wet branch at his sleeve. Plumbago, all its long shoots drenched. He plucked a flower and, without thinking, put the stem between his teeth, finding the drop of sweetness. She turned to see what had stopped him.

'Ah,' she said. What struck her, almost painfully, was the blue of the flower, which was exactly that of his eyes.

'Children still do that, you know,' she told him, thinking of her little lost visitors; but what she was looking at was the town-boy she saw standing up in him, all his roughness gone in the tender mouth and formal, angelic pose as the song poured out and her poor mother wept.

185

'Do they?' he said, feeling a little foolish. It had been an unconscious gesture. He had forgotten the drop of sweetness, or thought he had. Something in him had not.

Over the five weeks since his first visit they had settled on a favourite spot in the garden. It was here that she led him.

A balustraded terrace, much decayed and minus its urns, looked down beyond marble steps to a lawn. The left side of it was laid out as a chessboard, squares of black and white marble – the white veined with black, the black with white – of which some had tilted and others were split, with clumps of dark-leaved yellow-flowering clover in the cracks. Along one side was a bench, also of marble, in the shape of a sofa, with bolster-like arms, clawed feet, and in the panels a pair of plump-cheeked scowling cherubs. It was out of the sun but in sight of her hives, which stood in the lower garden beyond a row of scrubby apple trees and a giant mulberry.

'Do you mind?' he asked. But it was a formality; he did not wait for her permission, but removed his jacket and sat, heavy-shouldered and shaggy, in shirtsleeves and vest. His hands and forehead you saw, now that he looked so much like a workman, were scabbed from the sun.

After a moment she slipped her hand into the depths of her habit and found an apple, a Granny Smith.

He made a little gesture of surprise, as if the apple were special rather than the established opening it had become to their talk. 'What a beauty!' he said. He turned it in his loose-skinned hand, then raised it to his nose and sniffed.

She watched him take the penknife from his pocket, unclasp it, and very cleanly, cutting in towards the core, remove a crisp little green-skinned wedge, which he offered her on the end of the knife. When she shook her head, he slipped it into his mouth and very slowly chewed. She was conscious of the sunspots on his hands, the scabs; like her own, like her father's – the wrong skin for this country.

The way of cutting an apple too was her father's. It was

to see it again and experience the tender pleasure it gave her, that she had, each time now after the first, brought an apple for him. It was his reaching up that first day in the orchard and plucking one of their hard little apples, and sitting himself down and cutting into it, that had, almost by chance, re-established the continuity in their lives, and created, with an immediacy they might not otherwise have managed, this intimacy between them.

They had seen little of one another over the years. His place in the House, then later as a Minister, meant he had always been in view, but only in a public way. It was her mother, and later Meg, who had passed on family news. Then, two years ago, when one of her contacts was threatened because of the war, she had, presuming on their closeness, written him a letter, asking if he could use his influence with the authorities who, as she put it, were being more than usually stupid. It did not occur to her that it might harm him.

Her contact was a Catholic priest in Jena, whose work touched on her own, but whose doctorate, the backing of his order, and a university laboratory to consult, meant he was better placed than she was to answer certain questions that had engaged her for nearly thirty years.

It seemed absurd, she wrote, that the business of nations (these were early days, before the full horror had come to them) should get in the way of work that had only to do with *nature*; which knew nothing, cared nothing either, for the little laws of men – even statesmen. There was, she assured him, no code involved in the information she and her priest were passing back and forth; or rather, there was a code, but they had not cracked it, and she doubted whether the Commonwealth censors would either, unless they happened to be bees. She had no reason to believe her priest (however patriotic he might be – she too was patriotic, up to a point) was any more dangerous as a German, and a Roman, than she was as an Australian and a mere woman and nun . . . All this in a hasty, rather untidy hand, and all of it evocative enough of what he had known of her over the years to make him smile at the bossiness, the mixture of appeal to his power and large-handed dismissal of its sphere.

He kept it by him and read it again, not much interested, frankly, in the problem, but to get the quality of her, which was so tart on the page, and which took him back to his boyish self, and her, and all that time of painful beginnings.

He did reopen the way to her alien contact, then wrote in a more personal way to say that he had heard of her work, which was not quite so obscure as she believed, and how pleased her mother and father would have been – it seemed strange, after so long, to recall these guardian figures, these ghosts of a lifetime ago – and went on, having evoked the spirit of family, to a private matter, the death of his wife, which had occurred just seven months before. He wondered if he might come one day and visit her. Did the order permit that? Only, of course, if it was permissible and she herself did not mind.

She was surprised, reading his letter, by its courtesy, its tentativeness, its tenderness she might have said, and recalling her own prickly tone felt foolish; all the more because she knew it had less to do with the offence to her pride in having to beg than with her feelings for *him*, which were still, after so long, quite raw and unresolved.

She read and reread his letter, and meant to reply but did not. A whole year went by. Till one morning she opened the newspaper and found herself swept up in a storm of public anger, and accusation and denial, that meant they *had* to meet, but no longer on their own terms.

A Fortitude Valley pastry cook, Walter Goetz by name, a

naturalised German, had had his windows broken the week after Paschendaele by a gang of patriotic football fans. When he complained he was himself arrested, charged with disturbing the peace, and found guilty. He and his Australian wife and four children were to be deported and their assets confiscated.

It was an ugly affair. Protest meetings were called at which inflammatory statements were made, editorials appeared, one or two men in high places, who put their names to a petition, were pointed to and pilloried. One of these was Walter Goetz's representative, a Minister of the Crown no less, Lachlan Beattie. He was attacked in Parliament, there was a break-in at his home, someone in his own office leaked documents to the press, and among them was a letter from a nun, Sister Monica, who turned out to be Mr Beattie's cousin, appealing, etc, etc. Sister Monica, Janet, was astonished one morning to find her letters to Father Elsheimer reproduced in all their dangerous mystery on the front page of *The Courier*, flight-patterns, dance-steps, points of the compass, all explicable now as the language of an international conspiracy. Most damning of all was her letter to her cousin.

Rereading it in cold print, she did find it odd. Its tone was provocative, no doubt of that, and seen in a public rather than a personal light, rather puzzling; even she had to admit that. Within an hour he had called on the telephone to apologise and reassure her. The affair really involved only himself. He was sorry she had been dragged into it. But she was ashamed. She saw at once the seriousness of the thing.

The other nuns, caught up in the excitement of it, did not; till other calls began to come in: newspapers demanding interviews, parents cancelling music lessons, anonymous voices shouting loyal obscenities. A youth on a bicycle rode up the drive, a butcher's boy it turned out, and put a stone through one of their windows wrapped in a Union Jack.

In the afternoons after school was out, half a dozen local children, rather ragged and barefoot, the girls and boys both, had been accustomed to come with shoe-boxes under their arm and pick mulberry leaves. They were poor children from one-roomed shacks on Wynnum Road. Their mothers took in washing. Their fathers worked at the abattoirs at Cannon Hills or were labourers on the roads. Sister Monica had let them scramble up high after the tenderest leaves and given them beeswax to chew. When all the sweetness was gone and the wax was white, they would mould it into miniature chairs and tables for their dolls' houses, and the boys, these days, into tanks, which they brought to show her. 'Baroom!' Now they were forbidden the place. In half a dozen houses all along Wynnum Road there was wailing as silkworms starved and fathers set off in search of alternative mulberry trees. Ridiculous, all of it! At the end of the week Lachlan Beattie telephoned again and, on Mother Francis' suggestion, made his first visit.

They had faced one another on that occasion with a certain shyness. It would have been difficult anyway, after so long. In some ways the 'circumstances' made it easier; they could start off with something public between them. She apologised again for having embarrassed him.

'No, no, you mustn't,' he insisted. 'I'm the one who should apologise. You're being dragged in my wake – you, poor Goetz. All that has nothing to do with it. Even the war. They don't care about that. They want my head, that's all.' She looked at it. It was fine, familiar. 'And they'll get it too, that's what I've come to warn you of – eventually. When it happens,' he looked amused, 'you mustn't think that you were to blame.'

'But is there nothing you can do?'

'Yes – I can fight, I'm doing that right now. I'll give as

190

good as I get. I'm no saint myself when it comes to that sort of thing. But I won't win. I've embarrassed the Government, that's the real issue. It's my colleagues who'll get rid of me . . . We might as well drop this, you know. I'd rather talk about something cleaner. Your bees, for instance. Let's talk about your clean little bees.'

'Cruel little bees,' she corrected. 'Oh clean too, yes – but there's nothing noble about them, or difficult, or unpredictable. That's why they're so easy to handle. And Mr Goetz?'

He shook his head.

'Was he a friend?'

'No. He's rather an unattractive fellow really, I don't quite trust him. The wife is all nerves. Sick, I mean. They're helpless, hopeless people. Nancy – ' He paused, but she knew who Nancy was – 'used to go there. She was fond of his Gügelhopf. So really,' he said, after a little pause – they were running out of steam – 'that's the end of it.'

They were walking down to look at her hives, and as they passed through the scrubby orchard he reached up for an apple. 'May I?' he asked. 'Will they mind?', and pulled one. It was ripe enough but small and misshapen. He slipped it into a pocket.

She showed him her hives, which were not of the usual sort but of glass so that an observer could see through to all that was going on in them, all the events and organised procedures and rituals of another life.

Like one of her children, Alice or Kevin or Ben, who loved to look in and see if they couldn't catch some bit of information that she might have overlooked (they too were on the track of the Great Secret), he squatted, peered in through the transparent pane, and his face, she saw, had the same puzzled wonder and wide-eyed, dreamy calm that she looked for in the children, being pleased, for a time, to give up the greater study for this lesser and no less touching one.

It was like peering through into the City of God – that is

191

how she thought of it, and how she saw it reflected in them; into the life of little furry-headed angels with a flair for geometry, and some power (this was the great Problem she had set herself) of *communicating*. The form of it was plainly visible, she knew, each time she came to the glass, but her mind in its human shape could not grasp it, though there had been a moment, long ago, when she *had* known it, of this she was convinced.

This, all those years ago, was what Mrs Hutchence had led her to. Not by explanation but through example and sympathy, which was why she made no attempt now to tell him what her life was but to let him look into the hive and see.

She would have thought of it once, the many-minded, one-minded swarm, as an angel. She thought of it these days as a machine, which was a change but not a difference. Would he understand any of this? She wanted him to.

That they had, anyway, moved closer, was proved a little later, when they settled for the first time on the seat beside the chessboard, and he took off his jacket, then drew the apple from one pocket and a little penknife from the other. What he spoke of, as she watched him cut and lift out a neat wedge, was his grandson, Willie, who ten months before had been killed in France. The penknife was his. It was of yellowed ivory, with a silver-framed portrait on one side of King Edward, on the other of Alexandra. He had had it as a boy, and it had been with him, still a boy, when he fell, among the contents of his pocket along with Woodbines, a box of matches, and a hard little apple he must have picked in an abandoned orchard, with a single sliver cut from it.

She knew what he was telling and wanted her to see. The boy must just have had time to shut the knife and slip it, along with the apple, into his pocket. Cutting into the hard little foreign fruit, inwards like that, to the core, was the last thing he had done, very solemnly as his grandfather was doing it, before they were called forward. The sour-sweet wafer might still have been in his mouth when he was hit – his last taste of the world its greenness, along with his warm breath expelled to meet the larger, colder one of the autumn morning, then the rush of blood. She watched the scabbed hands cut another thin slice, watched him chew and swallow.

Each time, after that, she had provided the apple. Nothing was said, except for his surprised 'ah' and the slow appraisal. So now, on this fifth occasion, she watched him eat and he told her: 'It's to be on Wednesday. I wanted you to know beforehand. They'll give the usual reasons, poor health, you know, as if I were fair worn oot – ' He smiled at the bit of old Scots. 'Actually,' – he looked at her and laughed – 'I've never been fitter.'

He cut another slice of apple. It went into his mouth. He chewed. Then looking up: 'You know, I wish I'd come ten years ago.'

She caught his eye and was puzzled a moment, then saw what he was thinking. Now how was that? He meant he might have had Willie with him. She would have seen the boy.

But not more clearly, she might have told him, than I see him now.

What he wanted in her mouth was the boy's name; to hear it spoken aloud, in the world, on another's lips. Now how did she know that?

What a thing Love is, she thought. And that was the word on her lips, though she did not speak it. Love. What she said was 'Lachlan' and took his large paw in her own equally scabbed and freckled one.

He looked startled, she released it, and he sat, his hands in his lap, with the half-eaten apple in one hand and in the other the little knife. There was the sound of his breathing, a little broken, and further off the low, continuous humming of her bees, a note she was always aware of, somewhere, not too far off.

They had moved a long way back now, to a moment that more than once in these last weeks had risen up between them and declared itself, and been turned away. A scorching summer afternoon when the whole landscape around had been in shimmering motion, dissolving, re-forming, and they had stood together, he, Meg and herself – he a little in front, being a boy, a man – while the creature, unrecognised and unnamed as yet, that had launched itself out of the unknown world towards them, that the landscape itself had hurled into their midst, a ragged fragment of itself, or of its history or their own, some part of it that was still to come, had hung there against the pulsing sky as if undecided as yet which way to move, upward in flight into the sun or, as some imbalance in its own body, its heart perhaps, drew it, or the earth, or the power of their gazing, downward to where they stood rooted, its toes meanwhile hooked over the peeled bark of the fence rail, the muscles of its stringy feet tensed, its stick-like arms flailing.

She stood there again and found herself saying: 'I sometimes think that that was all I ever knew of him: what struck me in that moment before I knew him at all. When he was up there' (she saw the hooked toes again, dusty and misshapen, the muscles of his scraggy neck where the head was thrown back), 'before he fell, poor fellow, and became just – there's nothing clear in my head of what he might have been before that, and afterwards he was just Gemmy, someone we loved.'

Loved. The word, which she had used as if there was nothing problematical in naming thus such a tumult of feelings, released a weight in him that he felt shift and fall away.

'And while he was up there?'

'I don't know. Except that I have never seen anyone clearer in all my life. All that he was. All.'

194

He looked at her with his watery blue eyes, red-rimmed now in the blotched flesh, but the same eyes that had looked up, bold and fearful, at what was in the sights of the make-believe gun he had raised, the dry stick fallen from some ringbarked tree that had laid on the earth a season, dead, and which he had picked up out of its tree-life and refashioned, in their world, into a weapon with all the power of safety in it, of death too, and had pointed at the creature's heart, and *yes*, he thought, *hit it*, and brought him down, and that was the start of it, and so long as the image had life in his head, it was not ended.

She knew the end, such as it was, of the story.

Nine years after Gemmy's disappearance, Lachlan Beattie had been one of a Government road gang that was surveying the country to the north, preparing the way for a highway that would run, a thread of dust, through all the little burgeoning leap-frog settlements, sleepy harbour towns, gold-mining camps, scattered dwellings round a railhead or timber- or sugar-mill, between Brisbane and, fifteen hundred miles further on into the tropics, the last of Governor Bowen's little far-flung struggling ports; across canelands sickly sweet with molasses, rainforests, dried-out, sparsely-forested cattle country with nine-foot anthills, and a hundred flash-flooding creeks and wide mangrove-fringed streams. He knew the country up there. He knew a little of the native languages. He had been working for the past three years, first as a labourer, then as a foreman, on road gangs all up and down the coast; work of an animal kind that would burn away, he believed, the last of boyhood in him, and his exorbitant dreams.

In each place they came to, from odd natives who came out of the scrub to watch them set up their surveying gear, and peg and measure, and lend a hand at times if it amused them, and the straggling groups they met who were trooping, miserably now, from one camping site to the next, he made enquiries. Only he would know, she thought, with what emotion, what excitement at the possibility of coming face to face again with someone he had once been fond of; what dread too, since his conscience was not clear. She had known nothing in those days of what he was feeling. They were no longer close.

He did hear something at last, though there was no certainty in it. The clan it involved might not have been the one he was seeking. He had only a few words of their language, picked up from Gemmy and poorly learned, and the place was further north than he had estimated.

It involved a 'dispersal' six years before by a group of cattlemen and two native troopers, too slight an affair to be called a massacre, and no newspaper had got hold of it. The blacks had been ridden down and brought to earth by blows from a stirrup iron at the end of a stirrup leather – an effective weapon, when used at a gallop, for smashing skulls. The remnants of the clan, including the young woman who gave him his facts, had scattered and been absorbed into a larger group. The bones of the victims, eight or nine in all, men, women, two small children, they had carried with them and disposed of in the usual way, in parcels in the forks of trees.

The story already had elements in common with others he had heard up here, which when he tried to track them down had proved elusive. Perhaps they were all one story. Whether this one had happened, as the woman claimed, six years ago in her own lifetime, or in her mother's, or last year, it had been gathered now into the dreamtime of the land itself, a shadowy realm where the bones of facts had already drawn around them the skin of rocks, of beasts, of air.

The young woman offered to guide him there, and since she had been a child at the time, ten or eleven, they took an older woman with them; but she too, when questioned, was vague and would lead him only by indirections. It was he who felt a kind of certainty and clung to it, as they struck away from the coast and came at last to a bit of scrub by a waterhole. The two women squatted behind a rock. They refused to go further. The older woman began to wail.

There were bones – not so many. Eight parcels of bark, two of child size, resting a little above eye-level.

He looked at one dry bundle, then another – they were not distinguishable – and felt nothing more for one than for any of them. His feelings, which had seemed so clear as they approached the place, failed him now. He sorrowed quietly for all, in the hope that it might also cover *his* bones, if they were here, and decided, without proof, out of a need to free himself at last of a duty he had undertaken, a promise made, and a weight on his heart, that this was the place and that one of these parcels, which could not be disturbed, contained the bones of a man with a jawbone different from the rest, enlarged joints, the mark of an old break on the left leg, whose wandering at last had come to an end, and this was it. When he told his uncle of the thing (Janet had listened without speaking, without meeting his eye), it was as a dry certainty, though she knew he did not believe it. He was tying up one of the loose ends of his own life, which might otherwise have gone on bleeding forever.

All that, fifty years ago. An age. They were living in another country. He could afford to admit now that it had not ended. Something Gemmy had touched off in them was what they were still living, both, in their different ways. It would end only when they were ended, and maybe not even then. They would come back, as they had now, from the far points they had moved away to, and stand side by side looking up at the figure outlined there against a streaming sky. Still balanced. For a last moment held still by their gaze, their solemn and fearful attention, at the one clear point, till this last, where they were inextricably joined and would always be.

*

197

Later, when he was gone, Janet sat in the fading light at the window of her room – she still thought of herself mostly by her original name, and the more so today, under the influence of her cousin's visit.

Her room was on the other side of the house from the garden. Her hives were out of sight here but they were not out of mind; her work went on, continuous somewhere in her head, and she was pleased to have in sight this other view, these flatlands that as they approached the bay became mud, and later, when the tide rippled in, would be moonlight.

Out there were the houses her little visitors came from: one-roomed shacks on low stumps, behind tumbledown paling fences or rusty wire; yards straggly with sunflowers and strewn with rubbish, old bed frames, a collapsed buggy with only its shafts visible above a riot of morning glory, lines of colourless washing, and in a weedy pile, old beer and castor-oil bottles, charred stick-ends, broken bricks.

Behind the squares of light out there her children would be sitting down to boiled potatoes or bread and dripping, and in a short time now, would sleep, and silkworms, in the dark of shoeboxes, rustling, feeding, would be spinning the sticky gold out of their mouths, the finest thread, and miniature tables and chairs made of white beeswax from which children – Alice, Kevin, Ian, Isabel, Ben – had chewed the last faint sweetness, and on which they had left, in the moulding, their giant fingerprints, would stand in ideal order in the dark of little partitioned rooms, in houses that had been butter-boxes.

It pleased her to let her mind drift so far, then further – out over the muddy, stinking flats towards the waters of the bay, which were not visible yet, but approaching.

Her mind, even as it entered the ravaged yards, the shacks, the heads of sleeping children who were forbidden for the time being to visit but would come back when all this non-

198

sense was over, the jaws of silkworms softly spinning, was at the same time stilled, dreamily attendant, beyond tinted glass, to the life of the hive, moving closer now to the spirit of it, to the language they were using, those angelic creatures in their world of pure geometry, of circles, half-circles, hexagons, figures-of-eight.

When she glances up again, for she has been dozing, the misty blue out there has become indigo; the first lights have been doused, though the houses themselves do not fade from her mind, or the children who are sleeping in them. The first bright line of moonlight has appeared out on the mudflats, marking the ever moving, ever approaching, ever receding shore. All this a kind of praying. It does not make a house any less vivid out there because she can no longer see its light; or the children any less close because they no longer come to visit; or Willie because she has never known him except for what she has felt in Lachlan, and through him, in herself, the wedge of apple in his mouth; or her mother, long gone, standing out on the hillslope in the dark, the dark of her body solid through the flimsy stuff, the moonlight, of her shift; or her father slumped at the breakfast table, the loose skin of her mother's hand, like an old glove, on the leathery back of his neck; or in darkness now, on the other side of the house, the single mind of the hive, closed on itself, on its secret, which her own mind approaches and draws back from, the moment of illumination when she will again be filled with it; and Mrs Hutchence who has led her to this; and always, in a stilled moment that has lasted for years, Gemmy as she saw him, once and for all, up there on the stripped and shiny rail, never to fall, and Flash slicing the air with his yelps in clear dog-language, and his arms flung out, never to lift him clear; overbalancing now, drawn by the power, all unconscious in them, of their gaze, their need to draw him into their lives — love, again love — overbalanced but not yet falling. All these, Lord, all these. Let none

199

be left in the dark or out of mind, on this night, now, in this corner of the world or any other, at this hour, in the middle of this war . . .

Out beyond the flatlands the line of light pulses and swells. The sea, in sight now, ruffles, accelerates. Quickly now it is rising towards us, it approaches.

As we approach prayer. As we approach knowledge. As we approach one another.

It glows in fullness till the tide is high and the light almost, but not quite, unbearable, as the moon plucks at our world and all the waters of the earth ache towards it, and the light, running in fast now, reaches the edges of the shore, just so far in its order, and all the muddy margin of the bay is alive, and in a line of running fire all the outline of the vast continent appears, in touch now with its other life.

THE WORDS GEMMY shouts at the fence in Chapter 1 (the seed of this fiction) were actually spoken at much the same time and place, but in different circumstances, by Gemmy Morril or Morrell, whose Christian name I have also appropriated; otherwise this novel has no origin in fact. F. T. Gregory wrote a brief account of Morril's life from which I have taken the three descriptions of local flora at the beginning of Chapter 14. The Herbert letters in Bruce Knox's *Robert Herbert: Premier* provided some of the detail for Chapter 18.

My thanks to Joy Lewis, Brett Johnson, Christopher Edwards, who typed the manuscript and, as its first reader, made many valuable suggestions, Professor Alan Sanderson of the University of New England, and my editors at Chatto & Windus, Jonathan Burnham and Carmen Callil.